BOA

EDITIONS LTD

The Tao of Humiliation

D0067408

Also by Lee Upton

FICTION
- ❖ *The Guide to the Flying Island*

POETRY
- ❖ *The Invention of Kindness*
- ❖ *No Mercy*
- ❖ *Approximate Darling*
- ❖ *Civilian Histories*
- ❖ *Undid in the Land of Undone*

ESSAYS
- ❖ *Swallowing the Sea: On Writing & Ambition, Boredom, Purity & Secrecy*

CRITICAL PROSE
- ❖ *Jean Garrigue: A Poetics of Plenitude*
- ❖ *Obsession and Release: Rereading the Poetry of Louise Bogan*
- ❖ *The Muse of Abandonment: Origin, Identity, Mastery in Five American Poets*
- ❖ *Defensive Measures: The Poetry of Niedecker, Bishop, Glück, and Carson*

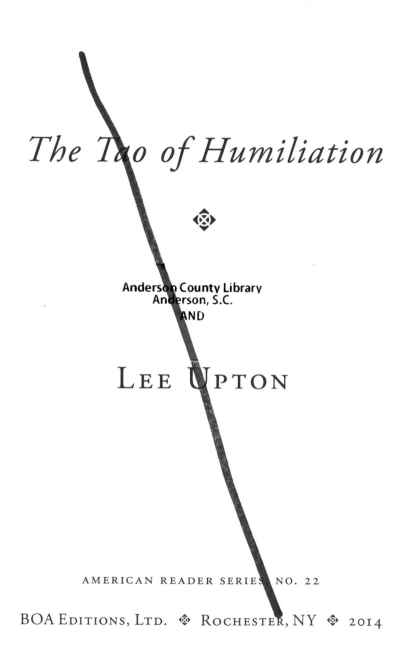

The Tao of Humiliation

❖

LEE UPTON

AMERICAN READER SERIES, NO. 22

BOA EDITIONS, LTD. ❖ ROCHESTER, NY ❖ 2014

First Edition
14 15 16 17 7 6 5 4 3 2 1

For information about permission to reuse any material from this book please
contact The Permissions Company at www.permissionscompany.com or e-mail
permdude@eclipse.net.

Publications by BOA Editions, Ltd.—a not-for-profit
corporation under section 501 (c) (3) of the United States
Internal Revenue Code—are made possible with funds
from a variety of sources, including public funds from
the New York State Council on the Arts, a state agency;
the Literature Program of the National Endowment for
the Arts; the County of Monroe, NY; the Lannan Foundation for support of the Lannan Translations Selection
Series; the Mary S. Mulligan Charitable Trust; the Rochester Area Community Foundation; the Arts & Cultural
Council for Greater Rochester; the Steeple-Jack Fund;
the Ames-Amzalak Memorial Trust in memory of Henry
Ames, Semon Amzalak and Dan Amzalak; and contributions from many individuals
nationwide. See Colophon on page 232 for special individual acknowledgments.

ART WORKS.
arts.gov

State of the Arts

NYSCA

Cover Design: Sandy Knight
Interior Design and Composition: Richard Foerster
Manufacturing: McNaughton & Gunn
BOA Logo: Mirko

Library of Congress Cataloging-in-Publication Data

Upton, Lee, 1953–
  [Short stories. Selections]
  The Tao of humiliation : short stories / by Lee Upton. — First Edition.
      pages cm
  1. Short stories, American. I. Title.
  ISBN 978-1-938160-32-5 (pbk. : alk. paper)
  PS3571.P46A6 2014
  813'.54—dc23
                          2013044056

BOA Editions, Ltd.
250 North Goodman Street, Suite 306
Rochester, NY 14607
www.boaeditions.org
A. Poulin, Jr., Founder (1938–1996)

Contents

for Alice Faye Upton

The Ideal Reader

Only three women are visible in that famous Cornell Capa photograph of writers crammed in George Plimpton's living room. Two of those women perch in the foreground, where they always make me think of sparrows waiting their turn while the blue jays flutter around the seed ball. Otherwise, the place is stuffed with men in suits, clutching their drinks like tabernacle candles in a funeral procession for the next literary reputation.

It's pretty wonderful that Truman Capote sits forward on the couch like a charming fat child. And doubly wonderful that the subject of my biography, Malcolm Alfred Kulkins, hovers in profile under a black-framed print on the wall. Was he taking his own measure, or deciding he was above taking his own measure in that room?

Triply wonderful: the tilt to Kulkins's posture as if he's ready to topple backward. Which would land him on Truman Capote. Not that I want any more damage to have been done to Truman Capote. It's the prospect of comical mayhem that I like—and the sense that at that exact moment Kulkins was a happy man and an eminence to be feared even among the raging egoists around him.

If you had known Kulkins when that photograph was taken, never would you guess that decades later his obituary in the *New York Times* would be so perfunctory. Never would you guess that his final years would be rendered less as a mystifying withdrawal than as a capitulation to the limits of his talent. You'd never guess that someone so brilliant and bold could be condescended to like that, and so briefly too.

Fast forward from that 1963 party in Plimpton's living room to Kulkins in 1976. From autumn through much of the following summer he carried on, in succession, affairs with three obscure writers. By early August of 1977 a crisis occurred. Pages in his personal journal look bitten into, or scratched by a nail. In the final weeks of the summer of 1977: silence. Not only no more journal entries, no more of his comical-steely letters to editors. No more reviews or occasional essays. Apparently his nearly completed novel was destroyed. Seventeen more years elapsed before his death.

During those seventeen years nothing was heard from Malcolm Alfred Kulkins again. Nothing nothing nothing nothing.

From the start, I knew I couldn't make enough headway in my research without answering the question: why did Kulkins, who was practically born writing, give up his art during the last years of his life? (At the age of ten, Kulkins wrote of his own mother: "She is a tiny little prig, with the temperament of a lobster." Later, in his journals, he called the urge to write "scalp ache.") There were questions about his effect on women too. Predictably, his romantic relationships followed the route of mania, like those of nearly anyone searching for some ideal. As for protégés—none. He didn't like followers, telling acquaintances that flattery suffocated him, a statement that, at least from some, guaranteed fawning.

About the women who were among those admirers: none had more impact than the three who came into his life in the most brutal succession. Leslie Orlovdor was first. Followed by Judith Anne Clemster. Finally, Seyla Treat. The pattern of his quick abandonment of women was already long set by the summer of 1977, the summer when Kulkins visited the little town of New Bethel. I decoded those visits not only from his journal but from the hazy accounts of former acquaintances who could offer little more than the names of the women and the certainty that Kulkins had been serially involved with each when, in May 1977, all three women moved into one house—the house of Seyla Treat. Does that sound as strange to you as it does to me? All three of them had sex with him, although probably not, so far as the documentation I've found reveals, at the same time.

Predictably, the experiment ended. During a period when young women faded away easily, Leslie and Judith Anne disappeared. Into communes. Or Mexico. They left New Bethel weeks before Seyla Treat's drowned body drifted to the shore of Torridge Bay on August 9, 1977. Seyla Treat: her published prose poems were devoted to the scraped-stomach lurch of nightmares. Those were the writings that gave her name a tiny luster after her suicide. She is now buried at Kelley Cemetery in the midst of what, through an Internet search, I determined to be New Bethel's strip of auto dealerships.

The idea that the final year of Malcolm Alfred Kulkins's writing life was the year of Seyla Treat's suicide was to be the most pressing subject of my investigation.

There was never any mention by Kulkins that Seyla had a daughter. And so the question of just what Kulkins might have thought of the girl has never been asked. The daughter—a woman with the unfortunate name of Flame—had kindly corresponded with me via email, and granted my request for access to some boxes of Seyla's that she hadn't examined, which seemed like such willful incuriosity as to be bizarre. Only recently the daughter had bought the house that had once belonged to her mother, and her mother's boxes of drafts and other writings, in storage for decades, had been returned there. Seyla's daughter said she would be in Baltimore while I did my research at the house during the day. I had made reservations to stay at the Best Western.

I MapQuested the address of the house I was to visit and made notes about the local businesses: a medical supply company, a consignment shop, and the Comfort Manor Rehabilitation Center. None of which existed in summer 1977.

The blocks through which I was walking were filled with one-story properties with cramped lawns. In the street a child on a bike executed slow circles, jumping from the pedals and staggering to a stop when he saw me. A woman bending to her curbside garden turned a startled face as I passed. And in the distance, dazzling, throwing up sparks: Torridge Bay, where Seyla had drowned.

A breeze, fresh and cool, swept in from the bay. The houses thinned out and sycamore roots buckled the sidewalk. It was a Saturday in May and the new leaves' rustling grew loud overhead. I thought of Kulkins's copy of *The Odyssey* in which his little sister's markings decorated page after page. It was my contention that those scribbles by his sister started his long affair with *The Odyssey* which he used, in cloaked form, to report on the Vietnam War and later on his lingering fascination with Patty Hearst, a sympathetic understanding that cost him readers.

The Odyssey, I planned to argue in my biography, was his inexhaustible fount, the disguised source for his fiction's marvels.

In one passage that Kulkins alluded to cryptically, Odysseus lingers at a magical orchard. At the moment when any fruit falls, the branch instantly buds, the bud blossoms, and a new fruit inflates, round and ripe and ready for the hand. Perpetually, the orchard replenishes. No less than seven of his novels reworked that magic in disguised form—and I was relatively sure that I was the only reader to notice it. In his own life Kulkins was like Odysseus on Calypso's Island: a man bewitched who ended his days without Calypso and certainly without Penelope. And not in the Mediterranean. Instead, he left all vestiges of the literary life to reside in Polkmedogt, Pennsylvania, in an old farmhouse where not a scrap of his writing was left.

Gradually the blocks I walked toward Seyla's old house grew longer. The area, full of two-storied homes at this point, was a maze of high hedges. Then the houses disappeared and the sidewalks crumbled. I could just make out how the ground darkened with marshland, sloping to the bay. A short distance ahead was the property I was looking for. It was the highest house in the surroundings and reared up for three yellow-bricked stories, windows glimmering. On the second floor a curtain sucked in and out like a drumhead. At each side of the porch four blue pillars rose, shiny as hard candy. The house appeared to shift, like a reflection in water.

With keys that had been mailed to me I unlocked the door and called out in case anyone was inside. Opposite the entrance, at the end of the hallway, a window threw sunlight across the wooden floors. To the left of the foyer emerged a dining room with an oak table over which hung a chandelier that caught more light.

And there on the dining room table—as directed by Seyla's daughter—were six boxes. And the boxes, undisturbed, were yellowed with tape. No one had cared enough to open them. Here in this room was the mystery of hands that had been lifted by a muse's, hands that Kulkins must have loved in his own way—and perhaps in the boxes there would be not only writings about Kulkins, but Kulkins's own writings. And clues to his silence.

I opened the boxes immediately.

In the first box I pulled out beads and feathers, plastic prisms with hooks, a child's set of fake papery blossoms thick with dust. Decorations for parties? Underneath, I found mashed jumbles of papers, writing slashed atop other writing. Unfinished work. Energy and hope, love that comes to nothing.

There were photographs between some papers. In one, Seyla's wide-set eyes stared into the camera, demanding something—what? And that wild hair! Her thick dark hair must have been as difficult to tend as an actual horse. And then my throat was closing and I felt my head filling with pinpricks. What was wrong with me? I hadn't known Seyla. But here was this box of gaudy little treasures—neglected treasures—and her daughter had unearthed the boxes that held these treasures, a daughter who had been orphaned as a three-year-old, who, according to newspaper accounts, had been abandoned in the house while her mother made a decision to end her own life in the bay.

I drew out more papers—crinkly onionskin glued together in blocks. Moisture, long ago, had seeped in.

Already, it was apparent that Seyla was ambitious in her own right, given the extent of cross-outs and the number of drafts. I was thinking as I looked through the papers that the discovery of a distinctive style was something that a writer was bent on. Wasn't Kulkins's discovery of his own best style—through trial and error, exposure to early and inaccurate translations of Portuguese literature and to the disorienting effects of gin—wasn't his discovery of a style the key anchoring event of his life? Not the external life, but the internal life.

It was a quarter to two before I had labeled the remaining boxes and made a rough chart of their contents. Three of the boxes held additional flimsy decorations. I put the prisms and cloth flowers and glittery ribbons into another box and made some headway with more preliminary sorting. By then my hands were streaked gray.

Later that afternoon, although guilty about it, I bounded up the mahogany staircase as if the sooner I made it to the upper floors of the house the sooner I could convince myself I had every right to be there. At the landing a door opened upon a room with a bed overlain by an aqua coverlet. Everywhere I looked appeared cozy and domestic and clean. What had I expected? To find Bluebeard's wives hanging behind each door?

And then, at the head of the flight of stairs to the third floor, an old-fashioned sitting room emerged from the shadows. From that room I stepped onto a balcony. Ahead of me spread the wide expanse of the bay, a faded blue. Within minutes the first signs of a storm brewed. The sky shifted toward gray, pearlless, without gloss.

Kulkins and Seyla must have stood on this balcony at the farthest point of the house, balanced over land that dropped down to the marsh. Here, Kulkins might have meditated on the span of his career. I knew certain things: he was the son of a mining engineer who held novels in contempt and a mother who resented her son. The most moving fact I had discovered:

his five-year-old sister's drowning when he was twelve. He was supposed to have kept an eye on her while they were at the lake near their home. That night Kulkins found his sister's white sandals in his room where she had been sneaking to scribble in his books. His guilt over his sister was something he never addressed in his public writing, at least not directly. I had found the pages of his journal that referred in coded terms to her death and then researched local accounts and discovered the drowning. Also found: a picture of Kulkins—a blurry shot at a picnic, taken the year after he went silent. He looked frail in the photo, even if there was still some of that life-saving mischief in him hovering just beneath the tragic cast to his eyes. He had endured, like a man who knowingly agreed to pay a price for something he was guilty about.

Anyone could follow the outward trajectory of his career as a comedy of ill manners and high volatility until the summer of 1977—whereupon after Seyla's suicide he stopped publishing. The general feeling in the industry was: he'll come out of this, and then watch out. After fifteen years there were comparisons to Salinger. The most loyal editor, B. K. Stringglot, hoped she could drum up interest via his silence. Over at Knopf, Jody Everley publicly wondered if Kulkins's silence was a ploy to increase sales if and when a manuscript eventually arrived. Other speculations: perfectionism. The will to outdo himself. His own attempt at retrofitting his style given the hordes of new young writers charging over the hill with their dinky minimalism.

I wondered if, in his final years, he could still feel pride in his early work, especially for scaling the peak of his own voice when he pulled the last sheet of *Monkey Grinder* out of his typewriter. Or was he prouder of the period I call

We-Climbed-Up-The-Mountain-Before-We-Climbed-Down-The-Mountain when he was living in logging camps in the Pacific Northwest, and much of his work read like the diary of an ax—repetitive strokes, the giant timber of one abstract idea after another crashing? Soon literary friendships spurred his ambition, including his strained and possibly fictitious relations with John Cheever. He referred in letters to meeting Cheever at literary gatherings where he could expect at best to be stared through or occasionally given an elbow. He was never sure if Cheever despised him or was engaging in horseplay—or if Cheever didn't actually notice him but was just trying to make his way through a crowded room.

Then there were the teaching appointments where writers were treated like pet geese, expected to snap viciously and mess the lawn. And where said writers ran through female students as if each were included in the benefits clause in the temporary contract issued by Personnel. Following those stints at the University of Michigan, twice at Iowa, once at some small Northeastern college he never mentioned by name, Kulkins found time during breaks and over the summer to return to Manhattan and write. Always, he loved jokes, tricks, wild goose chases. He got inside a critic's Manhattan apartment and slipped a mammoth salmon fillet in a desk drawer. He wrote a scathing review of his own fifth novel in the dead-ringer style of a critic named Barney Murteers. The piece was so well written that Murteers never had it retracted. His most elaborate illusions: Kulkins was known to organize scavenger hunts that no one ever, to my knowledge, successfully completed. As if that wasn't enough, he had a way of disappearing. You'd turn your back at a party and he was gone, not even just clear on the other side of the room, but utterly, as if it was a special talent:

disappearing. Practically everyone I interviewed mentioned that capacity as one of his gifts.

A thud echoed somewhere below, inside the house.

I sprinted down the stairs to the first floor. By the time I was able to reassure myself that no one was in the house, the shock had done me some good. For a moment, I wasn't living inside the imagined contours of Kulkins's life.

At four o'clock on my second day of research I slipped out behind the house. A haze hung over the bay. The wind picked up and sliced through stands of reeds. Soon my sandals were filled with silt. I wondered if the marsh had spread since Seyla lived on the property—and if she had walked upon soggy tussocks just as I was. I wound my way to the back porch, collapsed on a lawn chair and took off my slimy sandals. An echo vibrated. I swiveled. A shadow plunged at the screen door.

There is an odd moment when we first meet a human being we've only encountered in a photograph. If the photograph is at all true to the likeness, the actual living person appears to peel off from her surroundings. And between the photograph and the person there's a space that the mind makes, before the person becomes fully animate.

So it was that I thought I was seeing Seyla Treat. The person before me looked like the image in a photograph in the Austin archive, delivered with Kulkins's final effects. It was, obviously, Seyla's daughter Flame—with her mother's face, fleshed out, the deepest dimple above the left corner of her mouth. She gave me a startled look of incomprehension and apologized when she realized who I was. She said she hadn't planned to return from Baltimore this week, but "here I am." She said that twice.

"I just needed to get a sense of the view," I said, embarrassed for wandering around the property.

"This place—" she said, shaking her head, her hair in spirals, wild as her mother's. "Are you finding anything useful about my mother? Anything that you actually need?"

"I'm not sure what I'll find or how it will all work together." Of course what I most hoped to locate were references to Kulkins, jottings about him, torn pages of journals about him, possibly a letter to or from him stuck among Seyla's drafts. I'd given up hoping to find any of his own drafts in those boxes. Yes, I would look through Flame's mother's drafts respectfully, but with an eye only to what they might tell me about Kulkins and about Seyla's relationship to him.

It was sensible to be nervous about Seyla's daughter, no matter how much I imagined I should pity her. Biography, I had stated in my grant application, is one of the most demanding arts. That sounded self-serving, yet I meant it. You can ask a certain sort of biographer what his subject ate for breakfast on New Year's Day 1909 and get a detailed answer. The same biographer can't tell you what he himself ate a day ago for lunch. Casey Armitage adopted a British accent after investing twelve years in writing about the exploits of a minor British poet. During his honeymoon, his new bride woke to witness Casey—the biographer of her grandfather—writing the family name into his forearm with a razor. Then, too, there was the biographer who showed up daily at the Berg, her laptop wielding increasingly complicated timelines, and who began signing her name in the register as William Butler Yeats. Which wasn't even the figure she was working on.

If biographers could lose their minds, the biographee's executors and relatives were not infrequently the cause. Would

Seyla's daughter, the perversely named Flame, behave like those demonic executors who hoard the dead's words, who relish their ability to deny the right to reprint or—just before publication—withdraw permission?

"You're not really interested in her much—as a person, are you?" Flame said. "Are you really going to write about my mother?"

"I can't be sure about the proportion of the biography that will be devoted to her." As I spoke, my confidence was seeping away. How could I finish the biography even if I was able to answer the unanswerable questions that Kulkins's silence posed? There were so many difficulties. Getting a publisher might require the sort of luck my life had never granted me. Kulkins, after all, wasn't a celebrity, and his status as a literary figure had faded. And then there was the matter of Kulkins's own personal life. The way he ditched so many women—no, he didn't even ditch them. It would require planning to ditch a woman. A ditch takes time to dig. And now here with her eyes locked on mine was this woman who looked exactly like her mother. Who knows why her mother killed herself? Kulkins's other emotional victims managed to survive.

Flame turned away from me, but not before asking if I wanted to see the room she called her study. She did some writing herself, she said.

Her study was at the end of the passage on the third floor, a room just to the left of the one that opened onto the balcony. The first thing I had trouble looking away from: scraps of yellow paper flowers circling an oval mirror and lifting in the breeze from an open window. A mirror reflected a ring of more flowers and gave the illusion of garlands upon garlands rippling through the room. Loose petals on a bureau drifted before settling.

Clouds must have passed over the sun, and the room darkened. The flowers on the mirror deflated—and with them, dried casings and flimsy petals skidded across the floor. When I turned back, Flame was still holding open the door, her eyes wide and stunned-looking. At that instant she must have seen the room through my eyes, the musty interior, like the nest of a bird that gathered brightly-colored papery litter.

I was ready to back out when a bookshelf emerged from the shadows. I knew the spines, glossy in plasticized bindings. All of Kulkins's books. It occurred to me then that right there at the door, lifting her head, her eyes brimming with emotion, must be Kulkins's ideal reader.

Neither of us spoke for a while. Then Seyla's daughter said, "You're not going to write the biography at all, are you? You're just pretending that you're going to write it."

"I'll finish it," I said.

"No one will publish it. No one publishes anything that isn't sensational. So you'll have to find something sensational—or make up something sensational. A sensational discovery."

"That's not my intention."

"There's a beautiful poem by the poet David Ignatow," she said. "Do you know it? It's called 'Rescue the Dead.' It ends, 'You who are free, rescue the dead.'"

"That's beautiful. Really beautiful."

"I know. Did I tell you I expected someone taller?'

"Flame, there's something," I said. "Please."

She followed me downstairs.

The draft—lineated, unlike most of her work—was one I had passed over lightly. My fingers stuck to the paper as I lifted it from the box.

Angel of fire,
unchartered name,
child of the heart,
undimmed flame—

It wasn't a good poem—nothing Seyla would think of publishing. But it was an effort, direct, bald, that showed how nearly impossible it was for Seyla to find language to approach her love for her child.

Flame sat at the dining room table, the scrap of paper between her hands as I left. I was certain that she would not look through the other papers—in dread of what she might find that could cancel the longed-for words in her hands.

Flame and I didn't see one another for two more days, although I heard her moving around on the floor above me whenever I let myself into the house. I was finding plenty of Seyla's drafts but nothing that referred to Kulkins. Seyla didn't appear to have adopted any of his styles of writing or his choices in her career. She was, after all, that strangest of writers: a prose poet, a maker of miniatures, of voices lodged in ambiguous parables.

After another full day with Seyla's papers I began to feel as if I were staring into a half-frozen river. The longer I stared, the more shadows appeared, and flashes of red, and smudges. And yet so far her drafts didn't suggest depression so much as energy—a thawing, not a freezing. Seyla had given herself many voices, and her fluency read like health.

I was sifting through more papers when my hand jumped. There it was: an enormous cross-out, thick, canceling line after line of Seyla's handwriting. A huge X, like a giant spider, sprawled across a sheet. As if what Seyla canceled on the page mirrored how she would cancel her own life.

On that Thursday night, Seyla's daughter asked if I would like to come with her when she drove to see the property that her father owned at the end of his life.

I'm paraphrasing her question. I can't remember exactly what she said, given my surprise. I guess it had always been at the back of my mind that Kulkins might be Flame's father. I was on the porch, all set to return to my hotel, when she told me. Immediately I tried finding Kulkins in her face. We've all known families where the genes are piped through only one parent. All I could see when I looked at Flame was her mother.

"How do you know he's your father?" I asked. I was wondering how his paternity could be proved. His relations weren't alive. Of course I'd never have the authority to exhume his body for DNA. Nothing I'd discovered in all my searches could validate her claim. Then, too, I might have to refine my timeline.

Even as the calculations flashed through my mind I felt ashamed. If it was true that Kulkins was Flame's father she had been abandoned twice over—once by her mother's suicide and next by her father's neglect and refusal to claim her. Did claiming Kulkins as her father serve some deep need of her own?

All at once I felt as transparent as a glass anatomical model. As if Flame could watch my mind making its tallies, as if my mind must be cold and inhuman. For the first time—with the appearance of one small pinched line between her eyes—I realized the truth: she hated me.

In that instant while standing with her on the porch I hated her too—even though we had something in common, although I was far luckier than she was. I had intuited that she also wanted to escape her life. Wanted glamour and risk, even if vicariously. My own most stable memories: my mother and I settling down to dinner before the television night after night throughout my childhood, while my mother was drawn deeper into depression. As if even while we sat there staring at the television with chicken pot pies on our TV trays we were both sinking up to our knees in mud. By the time I was thirteen I learned to smile often—to reassure my mother that I wasn't being harmed by her sadness. Smiling was my small useless weapon. What did I do for my own escape? I read. In a sense, given that I had never known who my father was, Kulkins fathered me from the moment, at thirteen, when I discovered his novels and told myself: *In this moment, reading, I am changing my life.* His novels let me know that adulthood, when I reached it, didn't need to be a suckhole for misery. And so I read everything by Kulkins I could find. His literary mysteries borrowed heavily from fairy tales, but with sex, and the sex was gummy and wolfish and weirder than any that appeared humanly possible. Eventually I went on to graduate school and composed a dissertation on "novels of detection and the culture of paranoia." Afterwards, I returned to Kulkins's fiction like a woman rescued from an uninhabited island by a tramp steamer and delivered to a husband who never, despite the intervening years, believed she was dead. That is, I returned to Kulkins as if he were the ever-faithful one. Which, given his record with women, was ironic.

By the time I finished these thoughts, Flame had ducked back into the house without answering my question. I vowed that I would learn more—gradually, if she ever began to trust me enough to tell me how she knew who her father was.

That night I conducted a search through twelve of Kulkins's short stories that I had scanned and entered into my laptop last year. Even in that limited sample, forty-seven instances of the word *flame* or close cognates emerged (*fire, scorch—fire* usually part of a compound). Thirty-nine of those appeared between 1974–1977, from the year of Flame's birth until the end of Kulkins's writing life.

The next day Flame and I drove to the farm where Malcolm Alfred Kulkins spent his last years. The new owners had come from India only five months earlier. They didn't begrudge us for asking to look around. The woman at the house that afternoon explained that she and her husband bought the property in part because they liked the idea that a writer spent time there. "The atmosphere is very good," she said. She kept her eyes away from Flame and me. Her little girl, however, constantly tugged at Flame's hand before at last disappearing inside the house. Within minutes the child came out wearing a frothy white dress and white patent leather shoes.

The woman allowed her daughter to show us the path that led to the apple orchard. The little girl danced ahead of us, sending up dust devils in the lane. Again and again she stole backward glances, her hair fanning out prettily in a cloud.

The orchard was overwhelmed with thistles and high grass. Still, the trees had to be bearing. Apple blossoms drifted through the air. We were continually brushing them from our hair. To give up writing, to stop—even struggling, burdened with doubts: I couldn't imagine the prospect for Kulkins.

We were in the heart of the orchard when, dancing with happiness in her shiny shoes, the little girl climbed a boulder. The rock was hard up against the trunk of an apple tree, where no rock should be, I thought—as did Flame. That's where we pushed, working to shove the boulder aside, to see what might be there, what could possibly be there, what was hidden and what remained, while the child laughed at such hopeful strangers.

I called it a miracle when we uncovered the safety deposit box. It wasn't even locked. Inside: multiple drafts. Notes, un-dated. I didn't recognize any of the sentences, and so it might be late work—what Kulkins had written during those years when everyone assumed he faded into silence. After I caught my breath I made myself slow down enough to read a poem. Though it didn't begin as a poem. It started with what looked like rough notes for an essay:

> *The writer's lack of control, failure of concentration. The genie that goes to sleep no matter how many times you shake the bottle. Hatred of the writer: from other writers, from aspiring writers, from the writer toward the writer: hatred of the writer for the writing self.*
>
> *Hatred of the writer for his human muse, his desire to suffocate her talents—should his muse have gifts of her own.*

Immediately thereafter appeared the poem, with lines crossed out and reworked. It was signed by Kulkins. I had often thought that in his last years he might have turned to poetry, and here was my proof:

Fears—Not the Worst, Not the Worst, Not the Worst

To be alone
without money or memory.
To be inside a small love
when a greater love waits.

To be silent in the small love.
To hear someone beaten on the other side of a wall
and to be unable to
help or to
call for help.
To be able to walk
but not without being followed,
to be spat upon,
to return to childhood,
to write what no one
will read.

The air swirled with more apple blossoms, blossoms that seemed as alive as moths. We were in the orchard for so long that the little girl grew bored and headed back up the lane to her mother.

A flame of uneasiness shuddered at the back of my mind. What was causing this sensation? The fact that the soil around the buried box was loose and that we were able to reach the box quickly? The obvious fact that the box itself didn't look worn enough to have been buried long? Was it the way the little girl had smiled up into Flame's face?

Even more to the point: the writing was signed—and while the signature was a halfway decent representative of Kulkins's, otherwise the handwriting slashed across the typescript was not his, nor was the style of cross-outs. I had labored too long over his drafts in Austin not to know what they should look like.

Flame's eyes were moist and huge when I stood up.

"You wrote this," I said.

She flew from me, disappearing up the lane, this ghost of ambition's intrigues and forgeries. Enough evidence, I believe, for me to take her at her word: for whatever it's worth, to call her her father's daughter.

I didn't follow her right away. She couldn't just leave me there. I expected that when I walked back up the lane she would be sitting behind the wheel of her car, waiting for me. And so I took my time in the orchard where her father must have wandered, where he must have studied the apple trees, gnarled and stunted in the falling light, how with each gust of wind they shed the most beautiful parts of themselves.

The Tao of Humiliation

The guy with stringy hair was staring, which made Everett even more nervous, as if something was going on under the table with that guy. Was the guy nuzzling something on his lap—a field mouse? Or was it something else—a genital piercing? "I've been around," the nervous-making guy said, without provocation. "It's important to get around." His hair fell in two thin fronds from a center part. His name was Barry.

"How do you afford it?" a deep voice asked from the other end of the table. The guy who asked was Lucas, some sort of retired businessman who spent half his life in Florida, the cracks around his eyes like sunrays in a child's drawing.

"I come from a generous family," Barry said, pushing back strings of his hair. "They believe in travel." With that, he stood, and Everett realized what the problem was. Barry was wearing a kilt.

Kilts. Why should kilts be a problem? Everett had watched *Entertainment Tonight* and saw an old clip of Sean Connery in a kilt, which looked okay. But this guy in a kilt, this guy Barry—it was like a crime against a culture. Like he tore the kilt off some giant school girl.

When Barry sat back down, Lucas said, "I had the cancer." He spread his hands and looked around the table until he had the other men's attention. "I'm all right," he said, "despite the cancer."

When no one responded, Everett said, "That must have been hard." His voice sounded to himself as if something was wrong with his teeth.

"Hard?" Lucas said, winking at Everett and tightening his grip on a plastic bottle of Deer Park until the stag buckled under his thumb. "It's the waiting. Not knowing and waiting. And then you're going around giving the impression it's no big deal that you're dying. This featherhead—pardon my French—this idiot that my wife worked with—when things were at their worst she told me to my face, 'We all must die.' She's dead now so I shouldn't stay angry. Yeah. I know. I feel guilty about that."

"You killed her?" Barry asked. He dug at iceberg lettuce as tasteless-looking as a rice cake.

"No. Railroad crossing. She wasn't paying attention to signals. She's alive. So am I. She has to worry about that."

"I bet she does," Barry said, adjusting the waistband of his kilt. "You know, I can't remember the last time I had sex. That's a joke too. I mean the sex I had with my wife. Not the other kind."

Before anyone else could, the dentist named Dwayne said, "The sex you had with yourself." Dwayne seemed like he was trying to exculpate every professional courtesy a dentist should develop. He didn't even look clean.

"I lied," Barry said. "As a joke. I'm not married. That's why I have sex with myself."

It pained Everett when no one at the table laughed. He himself couldn't fake a laugh. Throughout his life he had paid for that incompetence.

Groups were about to harden. Circulation would soon be futile. Everett watched as Lucas, the retiree, scanned the meeting hall, clearly calculating if he should leave the table and set up somewhere else. Far at the other end of the building a wall was lined to the ceiling with antlers. Some racks were so huge that Everett questioned if they had been supplemented.

With difficulty, Everett peeled back the lid of his fruit cup. It was the kind of fruit cup that goes into unfortunate kids' lunch boxes. How is it, he wondered, that certain people find themselves together during social occasions, or at an office, or at a retreat like this one? And would he ever feel comfortable enough to contribute meaningfully to the conversation? Not that he could call what he'd been listening to a conversation—not quite. Something his uncle once told him kept him off the bridge to self-destruction: *Remember who you are.* A sufficiently vague piece of advice. Everett had played around with those words and their meaning for years. He preferred to think that the words meant: Don't remember who you *were.*

The staff member's voice, at least forty yards ahead, sounded like a mouse knocking around in an empty tin can. Dwayne and Barry were standing off the path, trying to make out the words as well.

Everett's sandal straps dug into his heels. Up the wooded path, other men carrying pails were stopping. Why did they all have to go clanging around with pails?

The staff member in a black T-shirt, bluish green tattoos twined up his arm (cobras?), was saying, "Gather them—they're for us—not for eating now, for later. Remember. Not now. For later. Watch for the pricks."

Barry, his jaw dropping, turned and whispered something

that Everett couldn't make out. The staff member continued: "The berries allow you to think about where your food comes from—and to work with others, to commit to the act of gathering in preparation for a greater gathering. Sustenance on a higher level. First, we think of our gratitude."

"Funny little buckets, aren't they?" Barry said. "I feel like a milkmaid."

You look like one, Everett was tempted to say. Heat writhed off the bushes. He could smell insect repellent high in his nostrils. The deer flies were supposed to be the size of hummingbirds.

The bush to Everett's left raged. It was only Barry trying to extricate himself, like a cat with a claw stuck in a drape. Barry set his pail down and asked Everett, "What do you think of all those antlers back in camp? I've been wondering: what if deer owned the place? Would they hang up a bunch of human skeletons? I mean, what do you think about somebody who needs to display so many antlers? I mean, I'm not like that. I ran over a mouse with a lawnmower once and it made me sick. The bone fragments were flying and I had to stop mowing. Do you think they killed the deer first or just found the antlers in the woods?"

"It rained last night," Dwayne said, edging over toward another bush that was so shiny it looked wet. "They're probably pretty clean."

Barry was still talking. "I don't know about this fruit patch thing," he said. "I mean, this is like manual labor. Are we getting paid for this? Although I admit it. I have learned something: do not go berry-picking in a kilt. They ought to inscribe that somewhere. Maybe I almost like this. We've been here only for—I don't know—not long, and hey, we're buddies. Buddies."

The heat was getting more spectacular. As if the men were stuck in a giant pot of jam.

"Your shirt should breathe," Dwayne said to Everett. "You're not dressed right. You're wearing cheap synthetics or a blend."

Barry stretched on his toes to examine Everett's scalp. "You've got mist rising off your head," he said. "It's like your brain is steaming in one of those Japanese bamboo baskets for bean sprouts."

Dwayne called out loudly, "Water—anyone got water up there?" Under his breath he said to Everett, "You're shaking."

"Maybe Everett is shaking with indignation," Barry said. "Other mammals besides humans do that. You know what's the most self-conscious animal? Other than us, monkeys, apes, and cats?" He clapped his hands. "Fish! Just kidding. Like anyone knows!"

Then somehow Dwayne was holding a water bottle out. Everett closed his eyes and drank.

"They're trying to kill us," Dwayne said, "from heat exhaustion." He was looking at Everett. "You in particular."

In the first light of sunset the tips of the antlers flashed white against the far wall of the meeting hall. Everett was thinking that maybe it would be a good thing if people had antlers. Maybe some people had *invisible* antlers. The lucky people.

As soon as Dwayne left for a refill at the buffet table, Barry said, "You know what Dwayne's like? He's not like a dentist. He's like a Komodo dragon. Komodos enjoy expressing dominance. They cripple an opponent and won't stop. The winner rakes the loser with its claws. It's like somebody wins an argument with you, breaks your leg, and then works you over for a half hour with a file. And that's not all. I saw all of this in a video. A Komodo bit a water buffalo and watched for fifteen days—fifteen days—until the buffalo died. From putrefaction."

At the end of the hall, one of the staff members was leading to the stage an old man in a plaid shirt and chino pants. A beam of late light, pink and orange, settled around the man's head like a fried halo.

"Forgive me," the old man said into the microphone. He looked like a talking death's head—like a yellow skull in an oil painting. "You've come here for help. For that I appreciate each and every one of you. The anxiety you live with, that constant anxiety—you're going to say goodbye to that anxiety. What I say won't put an end to it. This silence you're going to experience, these gentle tests of character, this fresh air and enforced cabin meditation sessions—all these will put an end to it."

Everett glanced over at Lucas, who was taking notes on a pad balanced on his knee.

"Because that anxiety isn't you. It's a tick that's lodged under your armpit and feeding. You have to put a match to its head. Or you have to pull it out with long tweezers. If I feel like hell today it's because I have reasons. Your pain, your sense of worthlessness, your despair, your self-contempt—those are things I can intuit. Your pain isn't only personal. Remember that. I'm not well today, and so I can't help but absorb what's eating you. If you feel lighter in a while, think of the Bible verse: the sins cast out upon the goat, upon the swine—and that's what's happening here, the weight of what you are, that's what I experience. You have to cast off your pain, burn it from the head down. You have to watch it curl and fall off.

"If I have the strength to appear before you, how much more strength do you have? Strength is gained by pitting yourself against forces that aren't hospitable. There's a little seed in your heart—"

Did anyone besides Everett find the reference to "a little

seed" embarrassing?

"There's a seed in your heart, and it has not been given the right conditions to grow. You have untouched capabilities." The speaker's voice softened. "What can I give you?"

Everett looked down at his own feet—long and skinny in rope sandals. They didn't look like his feet should look. A wasp landed on his elbow. Until the wasp lifted off, like a hostile little helicopter, he missed a few bars of the talk. He caught up with "These few days, these few precious days, allow us the opportunity to step back. Every activity is natural and reveals something of your nature to you. But remember this"—and here the microphone squealed—"there's something within each of us that must be faced. Individually. There's a depth you need to approach."

Despite everything, despite his own skepticism, Everett felt it—that extreme of self-belief hanging in the air, as if the speaker had found something that eluded every other man in the hall. Everett's eyes ached. The chord that tugged at his chest tightened.

"Some of you are afraid to see what's in front of you. You might see your failures laid out naked for you. You might see how you made the wrong choices. Some doors are closed to us. They were open for a while—but it's too late now. There's a shelf life for certain behaviors. The truth was revealed, but you turned away. You couldn't face the truth."

With that, a suffocating smell of decay rose in Everett's throat. He struggled out of his chair. He was able to make his way to the exit and around to the side of the building before he retched into the gravel.

When Everett returned to the meeting hall, the old man was leaving the stage, a staff member clasping his shoulder, applause thundering through the hall. Everett hurried to intercept the speaker. He was grateful for what the speaker had said—although it hurt like hell. The speaker was right: it was too late. Everett had made the wrong choice. The truth was revealed. He couldn't face the truth. The memory of his failure had come upon him even while he was puking, the memory as overwhelming as a hallucination.

As Everett was about to call out, the old man turned his head, his pupils shrinking into a chilled internal world. Everett couldn't speak, couldn't extract from himself a word of pained gratitude. When he got back to his seat he found Dwayne holding his head in his hands, his back pumping. He was either crying or laughing while Barry whispered to no one and everyone, "Aren't you glad you came?"

Nothing in the preceding hours had gone well. Everett had overhead Lucas stop a brawl between Barry and Dwayne when Barry insisted that the combined weight of termites on earth was higher than the combined weight of humans. Lucas had said, "Theories should be based on evidence. Did either of you count the human population of the cheese-making states?"

Now Dwayne was saying, "I have some ideas of my own. The Tao of humiliation."

"The cow of humiliation?" Barry asked, as they hiked past a giant oak.

Dwayne turned away from Barry and said, "I don't want to waste the required energy to begin to do justice to the amount of contempt I hold for you—but I'll continue. There are various emotional responses that I'm pretty familiar with. First: embarrassment. Barry, you're the big animal buff. You must know that even animals get embarrassed if they're caught, for instance, digging up something dead that they shouldn't have. Next: humiliation—that's the stage I'm interested in. The rich stage. The third stage is shame. You have to enjoy a degree of responsibility for shame. Not so interesting."

Barry was following this better than Everett. "No one enjoys shame," he said.

"Give me a break. There are people who wouldn't know they're alive unless they were ashamed. They're busy congratulating themselves on not being sociopaths. You should believe me. I look into mouths for a living. I know something about humiliation. People can't keep secrets from me."

"So why is it a cow?" Barry asked.

"It's not a cow. Tao. The Tao of humiliation." Dwayne exhaled hard. His breath smelled like skin pulled off a fried chicken.

"I don't know what Tao means," Barry said. "I actually don't know. I usually know these things. If you'd asked me about cows . . ."

"Everett," Dwayne said, kicking at the path, "will you help out for once? I bet you know something about the Tao."

Everett didn't know anything about the Tao, and he would bet that Dwayne didn't know much either. The only reply he wanted to offer was, There's a lot to be said for the cow of humiliation. But he thought that would be humiliating to Dwayne, so he kept silent.

"In India cows are sacred," Barry said. "Maybe our cows should move."

Dwayne ignored Barry and poked at Everett's shoulder. "It was like they had a microphone right where you were puking yesterday. It was magical."

Behind Everett the sound of voices died away. The path was thinning out, becoming invisible under pine needles. What did Dwayne mean when he talked about humiliation? Dwayne had the ability to be irritated, but he didn't seem easily humiliated. And Barry—he was so out of touch that he came in costume to his own life. Everett couldn't blame Lucas the cancer-survivor for ditching them halfway through the hike. Today he himself couldn't resist peeling off from the group early.

The woods were silent except for the sawing of pine branches. The dry grasses gave off an almost sweet smell. For a long time he walked aimlessly before he saw the deer.

The animal was motionless amid birches and pines. To brace himself, Everett rested his hand on the trunk of a pine. He drew away slowly, taking a step toward the spot where the deer stood, as if he could walk through an apparition. His memories dropped over him—memories of himself and the woman he had known since they were children. The two of them had come upon a clearing in upstate New York and saw a nearly identical sight as the one before him now. A buck like this one, with enormous antlers. What he remembered most was their looking together, looking for once in the same direction. He and the woman waited, while just ahead of them the animal's skin rippled. The eyelid flicked over the wetly shining globe of the eye. And now, after all these years, in the space where the deer was standing, a concentrated afterimage clung.

He was there with that woman—it pained him to say her name to himself—the two of them, suspended, united in a way he never had been, before or since, with another human being.

He held back, not wanting to spook the animal or break the hold of memory. Suppose people we lost could come back to us in time? What if their genuine arrival was only delayed?

Lisa King—that was her name, the name he had been avoiding saying to himself. She had such a common name she could be in all fifty states by now, if she were still alive, which was doubtful. He couldn't bear to find out. Back then she couldn't be in his car on a winding road without asking him to pull over. He had to walk back and forth with her on the side of the road until she could go for another ten miles. And yet somehow she made him think of Turgenev's *Fathers and Sons*, a book he read as a college sophomore. The major activity of women in that novel was blushing, their cheeks suffused with blood. So too the tips of their ears. If she was feeling all right, she could blush as profusely and disarmingly as the Russians. But then she didn't feel all right too often. Her skin was like cool glass.

The next memory blotted out the first: a dark room—a fish tank illuminated with a handwritten sign propped against it. *Don't feed the fish*, in magic marker. The feel of her cheek under his, cool and fragrant and then the shock again—the knowledge that he was not enough for her. And then the other memory, the worst: the sheet on the bed drawn back, purposefully, the way someone from another century might pull a curtain to show an impressive oil painting. *My Last Duchess*. He knew she wasn't asleep. The soft dimples at the small of her back, the curves of her on the white sheet. Her body looked doughy, unreal. Even if she was a small woman, at that moment her body filled the horizons of the room. Her body that he had loved—it seemed to go on and on, stretching to the ends of his sight, a place more than a body, stunning and endless, this landscape, this world he had known, this love of his life ever since they were kids. Like a shooting pain the woman was back in his mind, lying naked on the bed, posed for him to see her.

And what was Everett to do—to stand and witness—to see what a woman he loved would allow, what lengths she would go to as a way to demonstrate that he was not included in her life anymore. He had walked out, hot with revulsion. She had been lying naked on the bed in his friend's apartment. She had known he would be coming over to see his friend.

Gradually the deer, the actual animal, impressed itself more fully upon Everett. Its hide was mottled, diseased. Something stuck out from its side, an arrow, broken. At last Everett realized.

He hadn't known replicas of bucks even existed, but here it was. It must be abandoned from a bow and arrow shooting range. A crusty old model of a buck. That was all. He'd been fooled by a fake.

Except for his breathing, no sounds broke the surface around him. He headed toward a copse of birches that he thought he remembered. The grasses in the hollow were singed gold and white. After long minutes he shouted "Where are you?" as if the others from the camp were lost.

He didn't know what was more humiliating: to be lost in the woods or to be found dead in the woods and have the newspapers report that he'd been on a strength retreat.

It would be humiliating if a rescue party had to be sent out. He already had enough to be ashamed of, given the puking that Dwayne said everyone heard. Now: disappearing in the woods. Anybody who didn't know him would think he was deliberately self-destructive. But he wasn't. He wasn't like the woman he had loved who must have wanted to humiliate him. To get rid of him. She had branded him instead. At unexpected times the image of her laid out like that punched through him. He should have grabbed her and set her upright and shouted at her: Why are you killing me?

After more walking he gathered twigs, acting purposeful, trying to lose himself in the task. He took a birch's fallen branch and brushed off the loose peel. He put it beside other branches and twigs. He'd seen men at the retreat making these little overgrown basketlike contraptions big enough to hold a crouching body. It calmed his nerves to behave as if he had something to do—some bizarre activity like every activity assigned at the retreat. He walked in the direction where he thought he smelled a stream.

Through the clearing ahead of him shrubs swayed. A bear? They'd been warned about bears. It smelled like a bear. The air was broken into particles. The huffing and coughing of a bear. He crouched to make himself invisible.

And then, hurtling into view, saddle bags of sweat under each arm, his kilt lopsided: Barry.

"I thought I saw a girl," Barry said, looking baffled to find Everett.

"A girl?" Everett shot up, trying to tamp down his embarrassment. He could feel his face relax, as if slowly unsticking. He was glad to be found by Barry. Barry only noticed Barry.

"It wasn't anything. Something. Nothing. A girl."

"You saw a girl?" Everett said.

"Are we lost?" Barry asked.

Everett should have picked Lisa King up in his arms—he should have taken her out of that apartment, gathered the sheet around her. She didn't know what she was doing. She was sick. The friend whose apartment she was in was a reckless guy who must have put her up to it—being with a guy like that could have killed her. She was that fragile. Maybe she did it because she would get sick if she confronted Everett. Show and don't tell was easier. Maybe she was afraid of what he would say. Maybe she was afraid of herself and her temper. Maybe he wasn't the only guy that something like that had happened to. Maybe it's happened to every guy that's ever lived. He was so relieved to see Barry that he was almost ready to forget Lisa King. His heart was loosening, flopping open. If he didn't watch it he'd cry.

Barry asked, "We're not really lost, are we?"

To which Everett replied, "We just have to wait. Wait long enough and they'll come for us."

"You're sure?"

"Eventually they'll realize. We may have to wait a long time. They'll miss us."

"I don't know. I don't know if they'll notice we're gone."

Everett didn't have to think hard before he said, "They'll miss your kilt. It's unforgettable."

"Oh. You think so?"

"Your kilt will save us."

"Great."

"Or else it will get us killed. It's kind of shouting, 'Kill me.'"

Barry said, "I kept thinking I saw a girl. Running. Like out of the corner of my eye. Just flashing by. I think it's a hallucination. You know that guy Lucas? The cancer survivor? He's writing a book."

"Oh, yeah?"

"He says that before you kill yourself or maybe he said before you die—I can't remember—anyway, either way, he says you're hallucinating."

Everett asked, "Did he try to kill himself?"

"After the diagnosis. So he wants to write a book about how not to kill yourself. That's why he's at the camp. For tips. But you know what?" Barry lowered his voice. "I wouldn't trust

Lucas not to depress a clown. Although clowns are often depressed individuals."

Barry couldn't stop talking—about depression, about clowns, about how you can't go back into the past and survive the present. On the latter point it was like he was reading Everett's mind.

Neither man told the other, but they both hoped Barry's eyes weren't playing tricks and that an actual girl was lost or in trouble, so that the two of them, although they themselves were lost, could save her. They walked deeper into the woods. Their shadows fell ahead of them. Frogs were starting up.

By then the girl had run back in the other direction, far on the other side of the rushing stream, and could not have heard the men who would have so gladly saved her, not even Everett, loud with theories.

Touch Us

Iris and Jacob slept with their backs to one another, as if even during dreams they were headed in opposite directions. As they were. She had nearly died eight months before. It seemed anachronistic—to be young still, or somewhat young, and to have such a bad heart.

Only three months after her second surgery Iris and her husband had argued, which was a hopeful sign. Obviously Jacob thought she could defend herself. She was strong enough to stand up to him in the kitchen with the dishwasher hanging open and shooting steam. It was one of those tone-of-voice spats: You sounded irritated, and so now I'm going to sound irritated. During the argument she felt as if her ribs shifted. The pain was so great that she had to sit down immediately— right on the floor.

After that, she and Jacob didn't fight. But they did talk. They could always talk about almost anything. Except, lately, about wanting a child. Or about how she didn't want to be touched. She could never explain how something in her stopped wanting to be touched even though she loved her husband. Both her doctors assured her that she should be fine by now, despite residual pain. But she couldn't stop feeling that her body was a stranger and had long been a stranger. Now being touched in any way at all made her feel that she could crack open and lose herself. Which shamed her. Of course it wasn't logical, such shame, such an aversion to her body. And maybe that's why logic couldn't do anything about her feelings.

It was a July morning when Iris's sister Amy showed up at the door, unannounced, with her twins. Amy probably thought she was on a mission of mercy. Mercy, which required guerrilla tactics.

A carnival, Amy said. Just like in the old days, she said. You have to come, Iris. I'll be a wreck without you. Really. You're doing me a favor, Iris. How can I handle these delinquents alone? The twins stood in front of their mother, like miniature Praetorian guards. For once, they weren't wriggling and wagging their heads. They stared up at their aunt. Iris wondered what Amy had bribed them with.

It was hard to disappoint Amy—all that need written on her pretty, big-eyed, insanely vulnerable-looking face. Easier to please her than not to. Amy was the younger sister and wore the role without interruption, unless she could get her way by using other tactics. Jacob never liked Amy and that both pained Iris and was, somehow, reassuring. Amy was so pretty with her slow insinuating smile that years ago when Iris started dating it wasn't unusual for anyone she brought home to stare frozen with admiration at her younger sister.

Amy's boys, Ephraim and Tanner, were dressed alike in denim shorts and blue polo shirts, and usually you couldn't go for more than five minutes without one of them shoving his brother or locking his head under his arm. Just being around them you could break a bone. They were nine now, at an age where head-butting was regular behavior. Amy hardly noticed their acting up. Or else she seemed proud of how loud and disruptive they could be. They were still staring up at Iris when she realized they might not actually have been bribed to be good. They appeared curious about her, and their eyes looked a little frightened.

"Where's Kippers?" Amy asked. She peered behind Iris for the dog.

"Oh—a long story," Iris said.

By the time the fairgrounds came into view Iris was furious with herself for being pulled out of the house. So hard to stop pleasing Amy, although it was the path of least resistance in the long run. If Iris hadn't come along today Amy would have shown up tomorrow with an even more preposterous idea: laser tag or skeet shooting. Besides, with Amy you actually did feel you were doing her a favor, that you were needed.

They immediately came upon two double strollers on the fairgrounds, and each time Amy stopped to talk to the infant twins' mothers, as if they belonged to a secret society and were obligated to exchange code words. When the sky began to drizzle the infant twins were tucked under clear plastic, like blister packs, in their strollers.

Soon the rain ended and wet patches on the walkway evaporated and the strollers were unzipped. The sun was fiercer than ever, and Iris's chest crawled with so much sweat that at first she thought an insect got under her blouse. Most of the carnival rides weren't like the ones she and Amy went on when they were kids. These were serious. Apparently if you didn't scream while you rode one something had to be wrong with you. Maybe you were already dead. At least Amy knew better than to ask Iris to come with her and the boys on any of the rides. But then there was the funhouse.

"Maybe I should just watch you guys?" Iris asked when Amy invited her to join them. She was beginning to feel like a bad sport—and she wanted to support Amy, given that the twins kept whining, and the shorter one, Tanner, demanded to know why it was called a funhouse when it didn't look like fun and the taller twin began echoing his brother. "We can get out of the heat," Amy said.

Amy and the boys blundered ahead of Iris into the trailer. The twins were right, Iris thought. What's fun about it? She was inside what amounted to a tight maze of glass and mirrors. Between smudged panes she could see children swarming with their hands out. The glass around Iris looked as if milk had dripped on it. From somewhere to her left came laughter, muffled.

In the next channel she recognized one of the twins. He looked close enough to touch before she realized her mistake. His image was blurred behind thick sheets of glass and somehow a mirror was involved.

She set out again, holding her arms like a sleepwalker. She kept finding herself in the same steamy quadrangle with the same tiny handprints smeared over the glass. At last a skinny attendant in jeans led her out. There were cameras, she realized. The attendant must have seen her lean her head against the glass. Pain is like God, she thought—it's not visible. Only its signs are, and then only to the faithful.

Amy and the boys were waiting for her outside the funhouse trailer. Then the three of them went together on one more ride, and Iris hovered in the shade of a sausage truck. She was there long enough to remember one of the strangest summers of her life, a summer she had avoided thinking about for years.

When she was thirteen Iris was hired to babysit a three-year-old boy during the day while his mother worked. And because the boy and his mother lived thirty miles away from Iris's home she stayed at their apartment throughout the workweek. The little boy's right arm was in a cast. He often tried to knock Iris with it. As if that wasn't enough, she had to sleep in the same bed with the mother because the apartment was so small. The only time she'd been more miserable was seven months earlier when her father died and her mother became anxious and frightened, and Amy became alternately bossy or helpless, as occasions warranted. And Iris: the older sister who guarded her little sister and her mother. Iris the brave and stalwart. Iris, who hardly let herself cry at her beloved father's funeral. Iris, who babysat to bring in money for her family.

One day while Iris was babysitting, something miraculous happened. Carnival tents and rides were set up on the edge of town, on a high hill. She and the little boy walked to the fair to look at the rides. Only to look: she didn't have money of her own. She can almost see herself. She must have weighed less than ninety pounds—a tiny girl in white shorts with pockets, and in one of the pockets the empty wallet she always carried. Because of a heavy downpour earlier in the day the hill was slippery with mud. Iris and the little boy kept sliding.

By the time they reached the top of the hill the sky was drizzling. No one was on the grounds except for the men who tended rides. Those men, all of them stringy and scary, wore shirts as flimsy as tissue paper. One of the men—skinnier than any of the others and nearly toothless—pestered Iris to buy a ticket to a ride. She stood there, mud splattered up her legs. The little boy was so terrified he clutched her hand. She told the man the truth: she couldn't pay for a ticket.

Lee Upton

And then the miracle started. The man took her hand and motioned for her to get inside a ride. She and the little boy climbed in, and the dragon boat shot upward. Iris and the boy could see off into the suddenly apricot-colored clouds. As they soared, the boy huddled close to Iris. Afterwards, the first man passed them on to other men who lifted the boy into ride after ride and told Iris to get in beside him. The men's kindness was so startling and exhilarating and comforting. The thing that surprised her most: the men treated her like a child, even though she was already thirteen. She hadn't ever thought of herself as a child, as someone in need of protection and kindness. She and the little boy were together in this, but then, reluctantly, because the mother was due home soon, the two of them began to float down the hill and into town.

They were only blocks from the apartment when the little boy clambered up onto a stranger's porch steps. Iris followed and reached out to ease him away. She knew how he could swing his cast at her and shriek. Instead he turned and smiled up into her face. Just then a door banged open. An enormous man, like a bloated gray frog, rolled his wheelchair onto the porch. His mammoth head was sunk into his chest. He didn't stop shouting even when Iris and the little boy bolted from the steps.

The boy—shock on his face, his legs trembling—would not let Iris carry him home or hold his hand. Nor would he forgive her after that.

And then, within a week, the boy's mother set Iris up on a date with an orderly from the hospital where she worked. The orderly was nineteen. That's what he said, although Iris would wonder later if he hadn't been older. The orderly stopped coming around for Iris only after—his words—she "went catatonic" on him. She hadn't known what else to do, other than to play dead, to stop moving, to pretend not to hear anything he said.

Amy appeared at Iris's side, the boys right behind her, and announced that she wanted them all to go into the silly old-fashioned freak show. When they went on the last ride she and the boys had passed the tent. It looked cute, she said. Just one more thing. For the boys.

"All right," Iris said for the benefit of the twins and to help out Amy. "I'm game."

This is it, Iris told herself. No more after this. Not even for Amy.

Who was Amy these days, anyway? What made Amy kind and yet spoiled, tolerant and yet a busybody, vain and yet sloppy and late and smart and self-deprecating and needy and, under it all, wildly in love with herself? Some women had a certain sort of power they could apply at will. It didn't matter how they looked. They could be ninety years old and you still felt it. They'd joined forces with their own power. They might be surprised they had the power when they were girls, but after a while they learned how to make that power work in their favor, and to enjoy it. After a while they didn't even feel separate from that sort of sexual power. They thought they and their bodies were one and the same. They didn't recognize that there was a difference between themselves and their bodies. Or if they did recognize the difference it was subtle enough to ignore. When Iris's boyfriends looked at Amy all those years ago, those boys thought they were seeing all of Amy. And Amy thought so too. But Iris knew that what they saw was separate from Amyness, the way a door isn't the room it opens into. Or at least that's what Iris hoped. Because if we are our bodies what was Iris? Hadn't everything she'd endured taught her that her body has a life of its own and that she has the right to hate that fact?

Amy was actually remarrying her first husband in August. He knew what he was getting and wanted to get it again. And Amy believed he was the lucky one. For how long would Iris's husband accept that Iris didn't want to be touched? He knew what he wasn't going to get, and he still wasn't going to get it.

Gorilla Boy, The Cow with the Transparent Heart, The Three-Headed Pig, Snake Girl. The canvas signs were faded. Whole words were scrubbed.

Iris lowered her voice to warn Amy and said, "The boys don't look too impressed by the signs."

"I know. We should have stuck with basic cable. They think they've seen everything. But it will be cooler in the tent."

And it was. The sides of the tent beat softly, buffeted by breezes. The light bloomed as if under a pink and orange parasol, and there was a smell of cut clover. Amy and the boys headed toward a raised platform while Iris paused just past the tent flaps, the shade calming her.

She caught up with her sister and the boys yards ahead. They were alone in the tent—except for a middle-aged woman on a stage. The woman was turning in slow circles. Iris had seen a face like hers many times—at the pharmacy, touring through the mall, waiting in the doctor's office. Even the haircut, the cropped helmet sprayed into place, was familiar.

What was different: the woman wore a lacy too-short dress that looked like an amputated bridal gown, and her giant thighs were rumpled and orange, almost like the color of rind on expensive cheese, and the rumples there were deep, almost trenches. Gator Woman, a sign said.

Her skin didn't look like alligator hide, not really. More like tree bark.

The taller twin—that was Ephraim—was staring, his face hardening. Iris followed his gaze to the woman's sandals, the purple paint on the woman's toenails.

When Iris looked up she felt the woman's eyes on her, as if a fly stickily crawled over Iris's neck and traveled across her blouse and then down to the Capri pants that pinched her waist. She shook her head as if to make a fly go away, when what she wanted was to shake the woman's eyes away.

Because Amy was busy brushing something out of one of the twin's hair, at first she didn't see that Iris took the brunt of the woman's glare, took the full force and couldn't look away. There was no way for Amy to see that Iris could not keep from thinking that she herself was a cartoon monster, her body patched and sewn sloppily, her veins shining through her skin. It was as if Iris's body was being searched by that woman—and her body was shrinking, trying to hide from the woman's eyes. For Iris knew it. Someone loved the woman and desired her too. How else would this woman have the strength to stand, on exhibit, and yet to pour her stare, willful, unconquered, defiant, out beyond her body?

Jacob. He deserved better. Even before her first operation Iris was never accustomed to her own body, never entirely comfortable with it. Passing her reflection in store windows and not recognizing who she was or else despising what she saw. And she and Jacob—never touching anymore. What was the problem? She could not imagine what Jacob saw when he saw her body now, or she could imagine, and did not want to forgive her body.

If it would make a difference, Iris was thinking, she would punish her body for being weak, for making her breathless, for surprising her with failure, for establishing an agenda of its own—for being too slow and for being full of pain and etched with scars. For shattering and then shattering again. For never giving her a child.

"It's part of the act," Amy whispered. She told the twins it was time to leave, Aunt Iris is looking tired.

To her sister Amy whispered, "I thought it would be— cuter? Fire-swallowers. A bearded woman. Fat Lady. Cuddly types. Old-fashioned. Like a drawing on a bag of cough drops. I'm stupid. I've scarred the boys for life. Stupid me."

"Gator Woman," Iris said, making herself laugh until Amy laughed too.

At Applebee's one of the twins shoved his head at his brother. Iris couldn't even tell which twin it was. Seated, they were the same height.

"You hate my hair, don't you," Amy said.

"No—I just noticed how long it is," Iris said. "It's gorgeous."

"You think it looks funny."

"I didn't say that. It just—it looked like you must be hot when we were outside. I couldn't stand long hair in this heat. Your hair looks really nice. You always look nice. Great. You always look great."

A grimace crossed Amy's face before she said, "I should just chop it all off. Like yours."

The boys' lemonade arrived. Crushed strawberries lined the glasses. "Hairy livers," one of the twins said. The other twin pulled the straw from his drink and dribbled pink liquid over his napkin.

Amy was talking: "There's a woman I work with—you don't know her—she's pregnant and she's forty-three."

Translation: there's still time for you, Iris.

And then Amy went on, "We shouldn't have come. I'm really sorry. Stupid. I'm so stupid. You're sick and I've made you sicker."

On the drive back the boys wrestled and got their seat belts tangled. Keeping one hand on the steering wheel, Amy twisted around and shouted so loudly that Iris turned too and cried out to the boys, No, and then, Stop it! She swatted at their thrashing legs. The twins stared, their eyes goggling.

Iris could have slapped their faces. She could have bent over the seat and clobbered both of them. Amy might have plowed into the car right in front of them when she turned to scream at the boys before Iris started in on them. What was wrong with the twins—so rowdy and loud—and not so very young that they shouldn't know better. A three-year-old would know better. Iris felt the way she did years ago when a group of kids on the bus picked on her little sister. Except now she wanted to swat Amy's own children.

Her forehead was hot. Poor Amy, she thought, I can't take care of you anymore.

She wouldn't let Amy or the boys into the house. Amy nodded, her eyes darkening, holding back tears. Repeatedly Iris assured her sister she was fine—she just had things to do before Jacob got home.

Iris lay on the couch. The living room was cool from the air conditioning. She pulled a blanket over her legs. She hoped she could make herself rest before Jacob got home. Try to be refreshed enough to be a good listener. She could give him that much, at any rate. They could talk. She could tell him about her day and hear about his.

From where she was lying, Kippers' rubber bone was visible under an armchair. Iris and Jacob had given up the dog—temporarily, supposedly, until Iris recovered. They both knew better. Jacob delivered the collie to one of his colleagues who had children. She and Jacob would never get Kippers back. The idea was idiotic to begin with. Kippers would be a loaner dog—to see if the colleague's kids could be responsible for an animal before they got one of their own permanently. The real reason the dog was gone: Kippers kept jumping on Iris. The longer her recovery was taking, the more anxious Kippers had become, tripping her on her way into the kitchen, hurling his paws against her chest. Jacob was working such long hours that he was dead tired when he got home and didn't feel like walking the dog. In other words, they'd come to the point where even a dog was too much.

The entire house was too much—the rubber bone looked furred with dust. When Iris and Amy were girls their mother made them get up before eight on Saturday mornings to help clean the house, top to bottom. How Iris hated it. She wound up doing the dusting for Amy who always cried long enough to escape the ordeal. The experience had bred into Iris conflicting emotions—a distaste for housework and a heightened attentiveness to disorder. These days just putting dishes into the dishwasher got her panting with exhaustion.

As if from a distant planet the phone rang. It must be Jacob. He would be the only one likely to call at this time—if he was going to be late getting home. He must have taken the first-floor phone out of its charger and forgotten it on the second floor.

She threw back the blanket and headed up. It felt like there were several more steps on the stairs than she remembered. Maybe it was an illusion, but telephones did sound different if something was urgent. By the time she got to the dresser and picked up the phone no one responded to her breathless hello. The phone felt cold in her hand. She was tempted to lie on the bed, but she wanted to be in the living room—to come immediately to Jacob when he let himself into the house. She made her way downstairs, leaning into the banister.

She lay on the couch again and drew the blanket over her legs. And now she couldn't sleep.

The sensation started: an electric wire under her lungs. Every time she breathed she felt sliced. Like a diabolical force from outside herself, like some crazy stranger dipping a hot electric wire into her chest. After an eternity the torture passed, but by then the pain had worn her out.

Soon a breeze lifted strands of her hair from around her forehead, fronds of hair shifting with the breeze. She could feel herself climb a hill, her legs wet from the grass, her dress tissuey with moisture.

She was climbing higher and higher. She wasn't even aware of her breathing. How easy it was. Her feet didn't hit against gravel or slide. There was no pain in her legs, no strain. Rain streamed around her—like no rain she had ever experienced. The wetness was soft, and then her skin was being gently pulled and folded back. She was pushing her face into a warm towel that appeared out of nowhere, and then the towel fell away to nothing. The lids of her eyes closed, and yet she could still see.

The blanket had fallen from the couch.

As she emerged from that space between dream and waking,

Iris managed with great care to shift her weight and rest her right hand above her waist. She could feel the warmth of her palm through her blouse, the consoling warmth.

Relief flooded her, relief to be lying on the couch, alive and no longer in pain, relief to be awake and warmed by the balm of her dream, so much relief that—although she fought against self-pity often—she let herself pity herself. And her body. We're more than our bodies, aren't we? But if we're more than our bodies, then aren't our bodies defenseless against us?

What if she had always been wrong about everything? What if she should ask her body for forgiveness?

How much a body bears. Her body that deserved to be protected. Her body that was innocent, had always been innocent. She thought then of her husband's body. His lonely body. His faithful, lonely body that must miss her body. Her own faithful, lonely body. And in her gratitude she at last endured a stinging truth, as if she were newly aware of and repentant for a crime she never meant to commit, had been helpless to commit. She wept for how she had kept two lovers apart.

My Temple

The retrospective exhibition was in honor of forty years of my father's documentary photography, in tribute to the breadth and seriousness of his interests. Some of those in attendance were the same people I had met at his funeral. We were now celebrating what the exhibition catalogue called "a life dedicated to an art of consequence."

A window behind us was open—the heat was bad—and early evening gusts sent napkins fluttering on the table against the wine glasses. After a while I was ignored, and grateful to be able to travel the room and look at my father's photographs at my own pace.

I was staring at a sequence in a corner of the gallery when I saw it: my temple. It had to be my temple, although just a corner of it was visible. There were the same pink, winding staircases and, in the foreground, the same pool that I had seen all those years ago. The background was fuzzy, but clear enough—I too find it hard to believe, but it is true—and there you can see a woman leading a child by the hand, and I am that child.

There I am, walking toward the pool, my hand held by that woman, although at first it appears that two children are holding hands and walking together until you look closely. And in the foreground: the pool that held both my father's and my attention.

In the photograph nothing at all appears on the surface of the pool but, horrifically, piles of children's sandals.

I remember the temple with such clarity because that afternoon I lost my father. It was while searching the grounds for him that I came across a long line of flowering bushes, like a tunnel of bushes. When I gave up trying to find my father I returned there and crawled under the branches, breathing in drifts of pollen that smelled like nutmeg. Around me, white and yellow trumpet-shaped blossoms hung, and underneath my bare feet the ground was as smooth and cool as talcum powder. Through the branches I could see if my father came near, while I imagined I was invisible otherwise.

From my hiding place I watched a man and a girl in the distance, most likely his daughter. The girl walked behind her father, although the two of them appeared connected, as if roped. Every few feet the man turned to make sure his daughter was there. Watching them, I was sick with envy, although I wanted to call what I was experiencing a word that I respected: heartache. My father's—and my own—experiences convinced me that I didn't deserve to complain of envy, given the nature of the sufferings we witnessed everywhere we traveled.

Only a week earlier I had heard the word *heartache* when a British woman applied the term over dinner to how much she missed her children, and it was a word that made sense to me. It seemed like a medical condition; I had *heartache*, as if there was a space where my heart should be and that space ached. When I was bored after trips and came home to my dolls I peered into their arm sockets or the creases at their necks and envied how clean and simple their bodies were. Often I wished that human bodies were like that.

Right after the daughter and her father passed out of sight, scratching noises flittered inside the branches around me. The scratching grew frantic. Whole branches thrashed as if an animal was trapped and fighting to get out. In panic I scrambled to the opening through which I had crawled. It was then that I heard my mother's voice.

I saw the woman's flowered dress first, flowing over her knees. The woman pulled me up by my arm. When I stood I saw that her face was broad and bunched with gray knots. She had my mother's voice, even something like her intonation. But she spoke in a language I didn't know. Nevertheless, it was clear she was scolding me.

By then, my mother had been dead for almost two years.

A small crowd gathered around us. The men wore clothing like my father's—dark pants and short-sleeved shirts that breathed in the moist heat. The women were swathed in long dresses like silky banners that shook in the breeze. It was as if the men were the background from which the women emerged like brilliant watery flowers.

The woman scolding me was hardly taller than I was, although the power rolling off her was immense. She pressed her face to mine without looking into my eyes. She smelled like old onions, and vaguely like an Australian woman my father and I had met at a hotel that month. I twisted in every direction to find my father.

Soon the woman and I were passing into the bright sun, and then into shadow. I was passive, limply accepting the disorienting whims of an adult as inevitable. I had a habit of taking off my sandals and running barefoot no matter how many times my father warned me to do otherwise. Soon my feet started to hurt. None of the people followed us. Now it occurs to me to wonder if she had lied to them, saying I was her child or that she was in charge of me.

When at last the woman let my arm go, we were at a temple. The walls glowed in the late afternoon light, pink staircases curling on the outside walls. I was spun around and pushed forward. The woman's breath beat against the back of my head. Then, just beyond the tips of my feet, the temple pool flickered. As I stared harder, shadows crawled in the pool. Miniature breastplates that tiny soldiers might wear were moving just past my feet.

I wondered if I was dreaming, if I was really seeing what was there. The clouds moved off the sun and then I thought I understood. I was looking into a pool of turtles. The pool was filled with turtles, turtles stacked upon turtles, shining as if polished. And below them there had to be more turtles upon which those turtles crawled. So many turtles squirmed in the pool that it was impossible to see where one turtle began and another ended. Some turtles, like horseshoe crabs on the beach, were upside down and looked blown out from inside.

The woman pushed at my shoulder, shooing me forward. The pool turned black and white like pixels. I knew that I could fall forward and never stop. I pressed my feet hard into the earth. I stiffened, holding my ground.

It must have been a long time before my blouse moved softly on my back as if it had been pinched and lifted. There was a breeze, and I knew that, at last, no one was behind me.

That evening the lights from the parking lot shot through the edges of the window shade in our hotel room. My father lay sleeping in a narrow bed against the wall. He had a tendency to whimper in his sleep—my mother used to complain to him about it—and so he kept on the television to cover the sounds he made. The walls flickered as if we were in an aquarium.

From far below on the walkway a radio jeered. I remember not being able to sleep and feeling I didn't deserve to sleep. Who was I to complain? Nothing had happened to me, really. And yet I felt that my life had been changed.

Never once did I tell my father about the woman who took me away. Somehow I thought he knew and approved.

At the reception for my father I endured more strangers' curiosity as well as the kindness and sympathy of some well-meaning acquaintances. And then, after everyone but the curator left, I asked to be alone with my father's photographs. The curator allowed me the privilege with such courtesy that my eyes stung.

For a long time I studied the final image in the sequence. There was so much horror in the world, why would my father have set up his own tableau? Or was I the one who misremembered everything? Never did I see children's sandals in the pool. Did my father see the truth whereas my imagination betrayed me, or protected me?

As you must already know, I'm incapable of recording truth as my father did. To capture a child's face numb from terror. To let the shrubs behind that child fade off into the background while the child's eyes demand to be looked into.

My father often said that reality was worse than whatever he could capture in a still image. On that afternoon so long ago, had my father been dissatisfied with how little he could find as evidence of a greater truth? Had he planted images upon duplicate images to suggest—to horrify—to illustrate what he knew to be true and to make us imagine what we could not witness? Had he created an art of consequence? Had he faithfully documented a dimension of the truth that would otherwise remain invisible?

I stared into the photograph of the temple pool, knowing what I might find among those children's sandals—given that the transformation would have been so easy for him, so convenient for him. How could my father be guilty of manipulating both the visible and the invisible worlds?

I told myself again that my own life was slight and safe compared to anything my father had witnessed. Whatever I discovered about the photograph, it would not change the fact that my father had created an art of consequence.

Still, I looked at the temple pool until my heart jolted as if it had been stuck for years. Could I even remember my sandals? Didn't they resemble any child's sandals? They were ordinary, weren't they? Brown and scuffed and ripped near where the heels rub and worn away there into small pale circles. Why should my sandals be in the temple pool?

And yet, of course—of course they were.

Beyond The Yellow Wallpaper

> *It is very seldom that mere ordinary people like John and myself secure ancestral halls for the summer.*
> —*The Yellow Wallpaper*, Charlotte Perkins Gilman

How we exhausted her! Night after night, the woman lay awake. We peered hard into the pupils of her eyes. We clung to one another and breathed her breath. We stirred when she stirred. We looked into her wide-open eyes until at last our reflection wasn't returned to us and we saw.

Given our past experiences, we had so little hope for the woman. She was nervous, complaining (fruitlessly), self-absorbed, napping at all hours, waking to fretfully mention a baby. We couldn't understand why she slept so much. But sleep was, admittedly, an effect we often had on occupants of the room.

And then there was her husband. A physician and amateur scientist, he studied pond scum under a microscope, spied on the jumpy little planets and crooked hairs squeaking: life pressing into new constellations, into colonies of jittery beads (as if rain falls inside rain itself!), into tiny nests and twigs, looped as if roped, or as if a bird's nest were blown apart in a storm.

You would think such visions would make him humble, would make him see where others saw nothing.

Instead he paced the room, carrying the woman about like a doll, tucking her into bed, calling her his little girl, and all the while we thickened, some of us climbing atop one another to peer through holes in the plaster, climbing, some of us, to the ceiling. And what we lived with: a ridge of mold, a mouse's skull, another ridge of mold, softening raw and black, sinking into purplish and yellow and gray arteries behind the walls.

At first, there was no indication that the woman would be any better than the others: the tubercular-looking man who peeled at the walls before drifting into a deep sleep. Or the old woman who buried her face in her pillow. Our better hope: the architect who ran a blade across the ceiling as if slitting a giant cloud of plaster until his wife rushed into the room. Next there was a little girl who stayed behind during a game of hide-and-seek and—bless her—took a stub of charcoal and marked a vein along every wall. It was an escape route, a start.

But then the woman—this woman—looked at the wallpaper, looked and looked and looked, although she didn't see, did she?

It was dizzying to watch the woman tilting her head, to watch her spinning this way and that. Her eyes followed the paths we made in the wallpaper, paths that we hoped would allow us someday to arrive beyond the elms and past the hedges, beyond where the trout lilies grow. Beyond where the moths pulse, to where the oak breaks apart in soft rot, where every burdock dries and bursts like a key made of smoke.

Whatever she touched in the room came off on the woman's hands and clothes, pollen smudging her forehead, her neck, her shoulders.

And as she looked, we looked too. We stared into her eyes until we saw corridors stretch, arches rise, tunnels curl backward and split every which way. Tunnel after tunnel ran in all directions. The patterns were unmatched, a disaster, like a map of arteries tangled and clotted, more tributaries streaking away and splintering into darkness and still others collapsing and sinking entirely.

We stared and stared until one night we saw even farther into her eyes—into a narrow passageway, and little by little the passageway opened into a sitting room with velvet curtains and an antique globe and book-lined shelves. In the farthest corner emerged an opening where a staircase led to distant lower floors.

The room spun until we saw the woman herself standing at the top of the stairs. Her dressing gown was stenciled with a reddish-black pattern of long tendrils. In one arm she held her baby, her right hand free to open the stair gate, and then to grip the banister.

And then we understood. It was blood that crept down her gown. She was losing blood, the baby bundled close to her chest. Her breath came hard. She wanted air but could not breathe. She wanted out of that house she shared with her husband and his sister. Prickles needled at her scalp. Needled and rippled down her neck and into her arms. Still, she was strong enough. Even if blood soaked her gown, creeping downward, she was strong. Her legs were not trembling. Her legs would hold her.

Far below at the bottom of the stairs, the black and white tiles shifted. Shifted again, changing places. The tiles receded, dimming. Across from the banister the wall turned soft as a sponge. Then the wall retreated from her fingers. When she reached for it, the banister slipped under her hand.

A day later she will sleep in a bed nailed to the floor at the top of this old mansion, and despite the rising heat of summer she will stay in this high room of barred windows, metal rings planted in the walls.

Is a baby so new to the world in need of a formal burial? A baby less than a day old, its crushed flesh tucked and swaddled in a basket? Once they arrive at the estate, the husband carries the baby far beyond the gardens and the hedges. The soil deepens in a patch of coriander, and surely, eventually, the baby will only be a dream for the woman—for her mind is weak and she would never forgive herself if the baby's death weren't a dream. Let her believe the baby's alive, at least for a while, alive in the house downstairs. That's the kindest thing. And let her write on her little sheaf of papers. Let her tell a little story to calm herself.

But then no one had counted on us, how day after day the woman would crouch on the floor, her eyes following the waves in the wallpaper, the runners, the swellings where we crept for her. She knew there was something within the walls, there inside the walls where we bumped in our dumb show, where we were crafting our messages, messages she pressed against and followed as we wrote in fumes, in the fragrance of honeysuckle dipped in axle grease, in the smell of sweat-saturated wool burning under a steam iron.

We feared that what held us was stronger than the wallpaper that separated us from the woman. We would always be within the wall.

And we feared that a nurse would be acquired. How convenient to keep the woman on the estate that had so long needed a permanent tenant, away from wagging tongues in the city, where a physician's profession demands discretion. And so the woman would be with us, locked away as we were in the room where the littlest of us touches noses with her whenever she comes close to the wall.

But that is not what happened. This is what happens:

The woman works as her fingertips bleed and her wrists bleed more. She strips at the yellow wallpaper until every wall is bare. And we float.

We float and know that far back in the woman's mind her memory is uncoiling. In days she will ask to hold her child. She will demand to hold the child until she's answered.

To whom was the woman writing? How did she know we would answer?

Feathery scruff, thistle down, speckled caraway, poppy seed, milk thistle, the trout lily's disintegrating throat, the carp's scale, the waxwing's spot, gold blush on dewlaps, from the dust you came and to dust you will return, breathable dust. Sifting, foxed, disintegrating into spores, mold.

There's a gate by the stairwell and a lock lower down. We float past the gate and the lock. It is morning, and a mist gathers, cool and growing.

We know our way.

We float through mold, leaf, and loose soil, each of us bulbous and eyeless, softening near crumbling forgotten memoryless flesh.

Mustardseed, Peaseblossom, Cobweb, Moth. Fairy dust. Dust to dust to dust, dust of dust, dust of the old, dust out of books.

What Doesn't Kill You Makes Me Stronger

Anselm was in the bar with two other men from the retreat: Toby, a minister terrified of speaking in public, who was married to a woman who was having an affair with his father; and Dick, who worked in some secret capacity for what he called the cosmetic surgery industry. Anselm himself was in recovery from his father's death—which he tried not to think about—and a succession of bad jobs, which he couldn't stop thinking about.

To escape the camp, Anselm and his new acquaintances Toby and Dick had hiked to the tavern. All three had endured enough of the sessions meant to increase their self-confidence.

On the television above the mahogany bar squatted a sumo wrestler who looked like Alfred Hitchcock inflated in a milk bath.

"This place reminds me of a strip club," Toby said, craning his neck.

"For a minister you seem a little too preoccupied with nudity," Dick said. His head grazed a patch of buffalo hide nailed to the wall next to their table.

"You can tell a lot about a person if the clothes come off," Toby said.

"Yeah, like you can tell if you should get the hell out of the room," Dick said.

"It's authenticity I'm interested in," Toby said.

Dick sighed. Even in the dim bar light his prematurely white hair glowed. "What makes you think people are any more authentic when they're naked?"

"They can't hide much," Toby said, spanking his thighs. His bicycle pants gave off a faint light.

"Oh no?" Dick said. "Have you lived? No, you haven't. My bet is that the biggest faking takes place when people are naked. Women anyway."

As the other men bickered, Anselm brooded over his employment failures, all of which followed a clear progression—from tending the artifacts of the dead at the allied historical societies headquarters, to granting desires to the unneedy at a charitable organization, to serving, supposedly, the interests of residential and corporate lawns for Green Growth. The latter corporation specialized in treatments so ecologically criminal that a misapplication in one suburban neighborhood left sparrows fluttering around the bases of flagpoles, unable to lift off. Seven chipmunks ventured through a mail slot and were found in comas on the hardwood floor of a beautician's foyer. After hearing about the sparrows and the chipmunks Anselm left the firm. His current niche: freelance tax and investment adviser. Three neighbors, two never unaccompanied by dogs, hired him for matters less to do with their bank statements and investments than for reasons of acute loneliness.

By now, the barroom was bloating. "Let's have a toast," Toby said, like a stage drunkard, even though he hadn't had much more than foam to drink. Dick was right. It was hard to believe Toby was a minister. Not so hard to believe about his problems with his wife.

Anselm told himself that maybe soon he could leave his

obsessions about his employment failures behind. Maybe he could tell himself everything had been a choice. That's what some of the discussion sessions at the retreat had been about: choice. Besides listening to blowhards, the retreaters had swum in a pond, picked berries, and handled snakes. But nothing seemed as useful as this nonprescribed activity: escaping the retreat and drinking beer. Before long the three men would have to hike back to their cabins, each of which resembled a minimalist high school production set for *Annie Get Your Gun*.

Maybe, Anselm considered, his problem was that he tried too hard. Maybe he had driven colleagues away with his perverse friendliness, smiling like a demented clown. But was it all his fault? His historical society colleagues, what did they know? They couldn't date with accuracy a gallon of milk, let alone a muskrat's skull. *Seeking understanding through the scrupulous display of artifacts.* There were more authentic and chronologically precise exhibits on the walls of a Cracker Barrel.

As for his colleagues at Green Growth—they would crop-dust the Amazon, chemicalize the most fragile artery of the Chesapeake. And as for the Dream Your Dream Foundation—the witless choice of a name was the true key to any organization's secret nature: they dreamed his dreams for him. They scrubbed the light off the future—the future that once had gleamed for him like the inside of the bone-colored shell he kept on his desk when he was a boy.

"You from that yoga camp?" The words bellowed from the twilight of the defunct cigarette machine. The man who shouted them scraped his chair back. Hunched next to him was his spotter—a younger duplicate. Professional bar types, Anselm thought. Bar guards. Like dogs that take too much interest in their dog houses.

"It's not exactly a yoga retreat," Toby called over in his informative nervous-minister voice. "Some of the people might do yoga, but it's not a retreat *for* yoga."

The squat fellow said, "You look like one of those yoga guys. In those tight yoga pants."

The blood was leaving Toby's face, and his pupils over-rode his normally translucent eyes. What was left: Raggedy Andy's eyes.

Dick bent toward Toby. "Aren't those uncomfortable?" he asked.

"No. They're stretchy." Toby picked at the right leg of his bicycle pants, just above the knee. "Like a second skin. Dolphin skin."

Anselm saw familiar eyes staring. Astonishingly enough, it was Ray Trunkajar from Human Resources at Green Growth. A memory descended like an acid helmet: Ray Trunkajar at the sexual harassment workshop. Ray had emphasized his one piece of advice: always keep your office door open. Given that they all worked in cubicles, including Ray, where everyone knew if you unwrapped a cough drop . . .

"How's it going?" Anselm asked, unsure how he had managed to get over to Ray Trunkajar's table. Above Ray, mounted on the wall, leered a stuffed jackrabbit with antlers nailed into its head.

Ray motioned to a chair, the back of which appeared to be made of a coat hanger.

"Just wanted to say hello," Anselm said. "Acknowledge that we have more in common than anyone else. A shared past. I didn't expect to see you here."

Anselm meant the tavern, but Ray said, "Oh yeah, well, I do this sort of thing. A strength retreat—sometimes you have to take your own advice. I've sent enough employees to crap places. It helps though. I don't mind telling you that I haven't been pleased about seeing you at the retreat. I can't escape my past."

So Ray was at the strength retreat—not just at the tavern—and had been watching Anselm, possibly monitoring him at the campfire and at the buffet and maybe at the berry-picking session and during that snake-handling session when Anselm humiliated himself by shrieking.

"You've got a nice girlfriend," Ray said. He wiped at a circle of wetness on the table with his cocktail napkin.

"I didn't know you knew Janine," Anselm said. He felt better now that he could tag Ray as one of those single guys who fantasizes about other men's girlfriends.

"My wife's at a comic-book convention," Ray said. "I couldn't take it—not another year. My wife likes the superheroes. I tell her it's like being married to an adolescent boy." He paused dramatically. "I decided to try the retreat, and it's better than I could have hoped for. Quiet time. I'm becoming a convert. What about you?"

"I'm getting the hang of it."

"When I saw you I have to confess I thought I'd blown my cover. You're not going to blow my cover are you?"

"What's your cover?" Anselm asked.

"I don't mean I'm lying. I'm just holding back the Human Resources angle."

"Nothing's wrong with Human Resources."

"Give me a break. I heard you were terminally ill. But that was a long time ago. You're okay?"

"I'm not sick, Ray."

"The things people say. It's good to relax. I don't have to hear any complaints. I'm glad you're not dying."

Dying? Why would Ray think he was dying? Dying—
Anselm didn't intend to be dying.

Another memory crouched on Anselm's chest—before
Green Growth, before Ray. A memory from the Dream Your
Dream Foundation. After a few months a weird cushion of air
inserted itself around Anselm, a no-go zone, like he was a bub-
ble boy. Did they think he was dying—back then, even before
his colleagues thought he was dying at Green Growth? That
could explain a lot. Like the time he was stepping off the elevator at the foundation. Those two accountants who looked at
him like he was a male stripper molting into a skeleton before
their eyes. Terminally ill, Anselm thought. Back then it was his
father who was terminally ill.

A weird rumor—but a long-lived one. Someone said Anselm was dying. The rumor spread. From one job to another.
The looks his colleagues gave him were looks of pity. "Rumor
has a way of self-generating," Anselm offered.

"I don't judge," Ray said. "I really try not to judge lifestyle choices."

Anselm drew in his breath. "What do you mean?"

"Okay," Ray said. "I somehow can't believe some of the
stories anymore."

"What are you talking about?"

"Okay. Two things. Your health."

"And what else?"

It was a long time before Ray spoke. "Bestiality," he said.

Anselm had to think. Feasibility. Did Ray say *feasibility*?
He made Ray repeat himself.

"With animals?" Anselm asked. He laughed. Sweat broke
out on his back.

A memory again. The sexual harassment workshop at

Green Growth. The guy from technology services asking, with a straight face: Are sheep covered? Much shifting in the seats around Anselm.

"What kind of animals?" Anselm asked.

"You would know."

Why is it that whenever Anselm passed between store theft detection devices he felt guilty? He felt guilty now. He didn't even like animals all that much. Had Janine known? All that worry, all those days, months, years of feeling disrespected and disliked at work, and what was the problem? People thought he was dying and in love with sheep. He tried to fill in possibilities. Squirrels, rabbits, ducks. What is bestiality? Goats. Species across species attraction. More like one-way attraction. What did terminal illness have to do with it? He guessed that the rumor kept people from asking for the truth.

"Let me assure you," Anselm said. "I think you could ask Janine. It's not like . . ."

"There was the chicken story," Ray said, folding his hands. "Listen, I'm sorry. The stories were vivid. And your girlfriend looked miserable."

"How could anyone believe that? How could you believe it?"

"Perversions are common."

"Did everyone think I was—you know?"

"What?"

"Perverted?"

"I thought you were dying. Now you tell me you're not even sick. I believed you were terminally ill. What—was I going to deprive you of a pleasure that didn't hurt anyone?"

"Except for the chickens. Jesus. You must have pitied Janine."

"Of course. But not everyone knew."

"They knew. Bestiality. It's not a rumor that has limited value as an item of circulation." Anselm glanced up at the jackalope above Ray's head. He looked away quickly.

"An insecure attachment to human beings," Ray was saying. "That's what occurred to me—but I don't mean to say I believed it entirely. It was just there, you know. It was something to take into account."

A young waitress offered them all a ride back to camp, including Ray. Anselm sat in the front seat next to her, with Toby squeezed against the side door. Ray and Dick and some other guy whose name never came clear were crowded into the back seat.

Shadows flew at the windshield. With each bump in the road something tickled Anselm's chin. He batted at air.

"Oh, geez," the waitress said, tapping the rear view mirror. "Sorry about the feather."

A wave of panic swept through him.

The next morning Anselm stepped out of the concrete shower stall on the camp's rim and shook his arms as if they crawled with worms. He shaved, splashing the placard of instructions for employees to wash their hands, where a scold had written in black pen, "That means you!" Scolds. His colleagues at the allied historical societies had been worse than scolds. Staff meetings were like that Afghan sport where men rode horses and batted around a dead goat head.

On the path that veered toward the cabins, Anselm met Toby, headed in the opposite direction.

"I've got something I want to show you," Toby said, reaching into the pocket of his shorts. "Only if you have time. I don't mean to—."

"It's all right. What am I going to see?"

Toby gave a half laugh that devolved into a shy snort. He thrust out a piece of notebook paper with words on it: *It is no surprise that we struggle. An organ is needed.*

"Gosh, Toby," Anselm said. "I'm sorry."

Toby tilted his head. "Wrong paper. That was a draft." He pulled out another sheet:

> *Something is needed to raise our spirits. This building, as not all of you know, used to be a fruit market. Following which for years the structure was abandoned. It was lonely here—by itself, a lone building, this building standing in its gray siding serving nothing. Now an organ is needed—an organ to fill this structure with magnificent sound.*

Toby's eyes sped over Anselm's face. "Do you think it will do the trick?"

"I'll say. I was getting ready to donate a kidney. It's good. I can help you out with a donation."

Toby sucked in his stomach. "The money has to come from the congregation. They have to make the sacrifice. If they don't make the sacrifice they don't have ownership. I don't like that word, *ownership*. It makes me think of a car dealer. Not that there's anything wrong with car dealers. My dad's a car dealer."

"Isn't he—a minister or a deacon or—"

"That too."

"He sells cars and he leads a church? Pretty clever."

"That's not all. He's mainly interested in teaching people about self-forgiveness. It's very important: self-forgiveness." Toby was staring at him—hard. Anselm had to resist the temptation to tell Toby that his father sounded like he was the deacon of The Church of Divine Self-Interest. That Toby's father deserved all the indifference a son could muster. Except that Toby, constitutionally, wasn't capable of indifference.

Anselm tried to banish his hangover with coffee, but whatever he was drinking in the meeting hall tasted bizarre—like it was used in a specimen tub.

"Personal strength," Dick said as Anselm dragged himself back to his cabin. "It ain't easy. Too much lifting."

"What's up with you after the retreat?" Anselm managed to ask him.

"That's a question I tend to avoid answering," Dick said. "By the way, have you ever heard of what's called animal hoarding? You can't stop. It's a disease. It's not bestiality, but maybe it's close."

Even here—even here the rumor had followed Anselm. Thank you, Ray Trunkajar. Thank you very much. Bitterness flooded Anselm. For years the people he worked with had looked at him and seen a dying—bestialist? Was that the term for a practitioner? He was almost grateful to be hung-over. It dulled the edge. Except that being hung-over made faces look rolled in crushed nuts.

Dick went into a deep knee bend, popped up, and said, "At least I'm keeping my promises. I came. I'm socializing. She can't say I don't keep my promises anymore."

"Who?"

"Pamela. My wife. The poor unfortunate. Not her. Me. But at least my fealty to her ladyship is complete." He went into another deep knee bend. In a squat, he looked up at Anselm and said, "Women, they speak another language. It's like a language without—without words. By the way, we're all sorry about what happened."

"What happened?" Anselm asked.

"You know. Your past."

"I've got a long past," Anselm said. "A lot happened. Not bestiality. That didn't happen." Anselm thought of Janine. Surely she didn't think . . . A stray thought: she had always re- sisted getting a dog.

Dick said, "It's not true. I knew it wasn't. That other thing from when you were a kid. Your father. In the heart."

"He's dead—my father. That's one of the reasons why I'm here."

"I guess so."

"He died this year."

"So you weren't a small boy?"

"At one time I was."

"I heard that you killed your father in a hunting accident and never got over it. Which made you unstable. I said an adult who takes a little kid hunting deserves to get shot in the heart. I defended you."

Anselm's father had died without him. The home health aide called at 3 a.m. His father's bed was sopping with blood— as if he had come apart, been split open. The home health aide didn't spare details.

Dick was waiting for him to say something. At last An- selm asked, "Who told the story?"

"Toby heard it—from somebody."

Anselm's chest cramped. The story was unbearable. He hadn't killed his father, he'd neglected him. Didn't call enough. Couldn't wait to get off the phone when he did call. And now he couldn't stop missing him. Parents are always accused of neglecting their children. Some parents do. But sometimes, sometimes, maybe almost always, it's the other way around. He asked, "Did Toby believe it?"

"He's a true believer, what can I say? Not that he held it against you. He could probably solve some of his own problems with intrafamily violence."

"Somebody made it up. Why?"

Dick stroked his chin before he said, "One: entertainment value. That's some people's idea of fun. Fun fun fun. Two: explanatory value—it explains you. The weirdness, your particular brand. Three: it could potentially isolate you from me and Toby. But you know what?"

Anselm found it hard to concentrate. "What?"

"It made you popular with both of us. Whoever spread the rumor underestimated what sick fucks we are."

When Anselm finished packing and was ready to catch a shuttle that would get him out of camp, Dick came trotting back with Toby in tow. Both men blocked the door of the cabin. Dick must have told Toby that the bestiality rumors and the part about Anselm killing his father—those rumors weren't true. Toby was breathing heavily and wearing a shirt the color of a housefly. Oddly, for Anselm, looking at that shirt felt relaxing.

Anselm was leaving the retreat early, but the day was full of revelations, one being that maybe the two men standing before him by some strange accident of fate were the only genuine friends he had. His other revelation: his girlfriend. Janine. Holy Christ, Janine must really love him.

It was Toby who spoke first: "Tell us," he said. "Tell us. How long do you have to live?"

Let Go

For three years, lifetimes ago, I was an office manager at a credit agency. During those years, with one exception, I never fired anyone. Probably this was because everyone quit first. The pay was miserable, there was too much work for any person to do in any given position, and my superior was an aimless man who was slowly ruining us all. His office window looked out onto the street, and it was on the sill of this window, visible to every passerby, that he kept his balled-up hamburger wrappers. It was from this man that I received orders to fire Paula.

I wasn't supposed to fire Paula because she was lazy or incompetent. We kept on a lot of people who were lazy and incompetent. In fact, they tended to be the ones who got the most respect from the majority of us. I was to fire this young person, this twenty-one-year-old typist, because when she took her first vacation her replacement from the temp agency did an astonishingly better job and was willing to take over Paula's job. The girl from the temp agency, Linda, typed at what was a phenomenal rate, according to my superior, although I had never been a witness to her fast finger work. Purportedly, she didn't make mistakes either. She was prompt. To top it off, she brought my superior his hamburgers twice during the week that she served as Paula's replacement.

Why I eventually agreed to fire Paula was not a mystery to me. My superior made it sound like a solid business practice to fire Paula. Besides, he so seldom made a demand that it seemed unthinkable to argue for too long with him—although I did express my opinion that we should keep Paula.

Paula had been with us for just over a year. She was quiet and did her work. She wasn't late—except for a couple of times and then with good reasons. She sometimes got lost in details, that's true, and once she handed in a document that was part gibberish. But when she was told about the problem she worked straight through her lunch hour to get the report straightened out. She was, I think, entirely unremarkable.

Except for her brother.

For years, even long after I fired Paula, I would think of her brother and feel a surge of longing and confusion—and even some envy of Paula. In fact, on a certain level those of us women who saw him (he stopped by at least once a week to take Paula out to lunch) felt almost proprietary toward him. He and Paula had the same dark coloring and slim, graceful build, although he was considerably taller. But more than his good looks, it was his manner that was touching. He remembered everyone's name after the first visit. Without fail, he helped his sister put on her coat. He had a way of making his whole face smile, and then he'd turned to Paula with a wink, and for a moment you could see what they'd been like as a couple of little kids. It was obvious that he was the kind of brother who could manage a secret. It seemed certain that they had had secrets as children—silly little secrets that they kept and that drew them closer together. You just knew that he was the big brother who protected her. I imagined that he would protect her after she was fired too.

I suppose that seeing Paula's brother was so refreshing because of some of the things I had to do and say. For instance: I had to tell a pretty young woman that she smelled funny—so funny that people couldn't get their work done around her. Frequently, I listened to employees tell me about their gynecological problems because they knew that although I was also a woman I would never in a million years ask them follow-up questions, and so they could get the day off with only a small amount of self-humiliation. Along with that sort of thing I counseled someone with an ulcer who worked with a can of warm cola at her elbow on doctor's orders. I think she got an ulcer because she was such a good listener—everyone confided in her. For a while two pregnant women kept falling asleep while talking to clients on the telephone. There were harrowing things too: I had to barricade the door three times when deranged husbands or boyfriends came for the women who worked in the agency, and one of the husbands was our security guard. Worst of all, I had to pretend that I didn't notice when a woman from accounting came in with her newborn baby and the baby was missing a hand.

No one had warned me. It was a beautiful baby, and I said it was a beautiful baby. And there was the mother making hardly more than minimum wage, and there was her baby without a hand.

Presumably there is a way to fire people, but I didn't know how to do it.

It shouldn't be done right before Christmas or New Year's, I reasoned. I decided that the right time to fire Paula was three weeks after New Year's. If I had to do it over again I wouldn't have done it at that time because that's the time, at least in Ohio, when few people have anything to live for. The snow has been around for a long time and has a used, particularly defeated look. It begins to look unnatural, even though nothing could be more natural. And then you have Valentine's Day looming around the corner, like some sort of mean mockery of everybody. But, as I said, the snow is the worst part. It isn't even a color anymore—but an unreflective, dead, noncolor. When I had to confront my superior again to see if he still meant that I ought to fire Paula, I stared out the plate-glass window behind him, past the hamburger wrappers wadded on the windowsill. The snowbanks looked as if an occasional canon shot landed in them. That sort of bleak snow makes you think that nothing will change. Things will just break down and wear away at best.

"Are you all right?" That was Paula's question to me. She put her hand on my forearm. Her touch was gentle and hesitant, and I noticed for the first time how broad her face was, like a child's.

She had touched my arm after I asked her to come into the restroom with me. When I realized that she thought I must be ill and was asking for her help, blood shot into my head.

Of course I thought it would be best to fire Paula first thing in the morning, so that she would have the whole day to herself and so that her brother couldn't accuse us of getting the most possible work out of her before letting her go. I also thought it would be best to fire her in the restroom so that we would have some privacy. My own desk was at the head of an office of eight desks. Certainly there was no privacy there. In particular, I didn't want any men to see her being fired. It would be too humiliating to be fired in front of a man—even some of the kinder men. And of course there were men in the credit agency who had hardened their hearts long ago to women in trouble.

I thought that my firing of Paula should be swift too.

But this is the truth: although I had rehearsed ways to break the news to Paula, I can't remember a word I said to her. I was trying to keep my balance so that I wouldn't plunge my head into the sink.

I must have said something to the effect that she was being replaced because of the accelerating demands of the position she was filling (i.e., typist).

I braced myself for angry words—because even a quiet, passive sort of person like Paula can let you have it.

What I wasn't prepared for was the way Paula cried. Never before and never since have I seen anything like it.

There was no prologue. Seemingly no beginning. No snuffle or slow moistening of the eyes or blushing of the cheek.

Her crying was instantaneous and silent. It was as if water were spurting soundlessly out of her head.

If I hadn't been there I wouldn't have believed it: it was as if she had to be made of tears. Her blouse—a violet-colored flimsy blouse that showed the outlines of her bra—was wet with tears. As if she had to cry not only out of her eyes but out of her cheeks and out of her eyebrows and out of her chest.

I count it as a miracle that no one came into the restroom during all this.

I myself was ready to run from the restroom. I couldn't even see her eyes for her tears; her eyes were that puffy and her tears were that profuse.

And then I started.

I was crying—and I wasn't even feeling sympathetic toward poor Paula during those moments. I was only feeling physically sympathetic, I suppose. I was lurching and crying. I was in my tears, inside them, swimming in them, and all my sadnesses came up—things I can't mention here and would rather not dwell on. They came up not as discrete names or memories but as substances of some sort without features, as if my sadnesses had turned to liquid inside me.

When I finally gathered myself, when I could see again, Paula had left the restroom.

I walked through the back door to her desk. She wasn't there. Her coat was not in the cloak room. I ventured back to her desk, in case somehow I had missed her, and the big beige typewriter—we used electric typewriters in those days—seemed to be resting by itself, just waiting for Linda, the remarkable replacement for Paula.

Now I am going to move swiftly to another part of the story, the part where I come to see that I have been party to something like a murder. But of course it took me a good long time to figure it out, and once more something strange happened in the agency's restroom.

The next week when I saw Linda seated at Paula's typewriter I felt guilty. I hadn't paid much attention to Linda during the week she was temping, but now I looked at her closely. She had Paula's coloring, that was true, but not Paula's smile. Paula had a shy, embarrassed smile—as if she were apologetic just for being Paula. Linda's smile was a challenge. It was a smile that practically spoke. Her smile said: You are so stupid. When she smiled one of her teeth stuck to her lower lip.

On the very first day she only typed in the necessary information on three of the forms that we use for garnishing wages.

On the second day it occurred to me that there was something vicious about the way she looked at me. And then I realized the obvious: she felt pity for Paula—and anxiety. She was afraid that she would suffer Paula's fate. She thought of me as the sort of office manager who fired people easily and often and thoughtlessly.

As I recall it now, I made a point on the third and fourth days of her first week to stop by her desk. I even brought her coffee twice to show her that there was nothing to worry about.

Once, I watched her when she couldn't see me. She was looking into a compact of facial powder with such concentration that I wondered what she could be seeing. She squinted at her reflection. She actually licked her lips. And then she smiled at herself—a beautiful, dazzling, full-toothed smile that lit up her eyes, a smile I had never seen her use for any of us.

At the end of the week I actually found myself staring into the restroom mirror and wondering why I appeared to be a person who is easy to disdain. I washed my hands, pulled off one of the manila papers to dry my fingers, and when I was about to toss the paper into the wastebasket I saw something that made my heart skip: mailing addresses. Lists and lists and lists of mailing addresses. Linda's mailing addresses. They had cost us a fortune to obtain, and she was supposed to affix those addresses to envelopes for our new advertising brochures. She had dumped them here. There could be no mistake.

It had been a long day, and suddenly I was close to tears. Linda had left early, and so I retrieved the mailing labels from the waste basket and put them on the top of her typewriter. I knew that I wouldn't even have to talk to her about them on Monday. She would see the mailing labels and know that I knew what she was up to. That ugly smirk would dissolve back into her face, and she would have to contend with the labels and my knowledge of her perfidy—and her knowledge that I couldn't be viewed as an imbecile quite so easily anymore.

As it turns out, Linda had picked up her check earlier that afternoon (it had been processed because we were at the end of the month). We never saw her at the agency again.

One of the women in our office, the one nursing an ulcer, informed me that Linda told her just before she left us that Paula had contracted gonorrhea. Furthermore, this was due to the fact that Linda had seduced Paula's boyfriend after she herself contracted gonorrhea from her dentist during a checkup that turned passionate following a routine cleaning.

"But why," I asked, "why did Linda want to hurt Paula?"

About two weeks later I was able to figure something out again thanks to the woman with the ulcer.

"Did you know that Linda used to live with Paula's brother?" the woman asked.

I felt my breath knocked right out of me. With that information I could see that I understood everything. How better to harm Paula's brother than to harm Paula?

"He must have dumped Linda in some spectacular way, and poor Paula was the sacrificial lamb," I told the woman with the ulcer. "I bet he was polite about dumping Linda. He used his politeness like a weapon. That would make Linda want to kill him, at the least."

And then my friend with the ulcer said: "Guess who else is walking funny these days?"

Of course I found out that she meant my superior.

It was all miserable—and more trouble for Linda than it should have been worth.

This all happened so long ago, but parts of it are very fresh to me. Especially the firing and the way Paula cried. And her brother. Sometimes I felt guilty about Paula and her brother although I never tried to contact either of them to apologize.

Just this past year, believe it or not, I saw Linda again, and I still recognized her after all this time. I was visiting with my cousin who asked me to stop with her at a yarn shop. This was about ten miles outside of Cincinnati at one of those little malls. I recognized Linda immediately. She was standing under rows and rows of knitting needles of all sizes, most in bright metallic colors—blues and greens and magenta. A line of hand-knitted sweaters dangled from the wall behind her. She had a kind of washed-out look. Instantly it occurred to me that if she were a sweater she would look nice until you turned her inside out and saw all the loose knots and clumped spots.

She tried to sell me some angora yarn but backed off immediately when she sensed my lack of interest. She had a superior air, and so it was likely that she owned the shop. It occurred to me too that she must have been a fabulous knitter and had successfully changed her avocation into a vocation. I tried to imagine her reputedly fast fingers clicking the needles, but of course she didn't give me a demonstration. Her smile was much the same; one little tooth kept getting caught on her lip. At one point her hand fluttered up to hide it—even from me, an old nobody.

And then a month later—this is the way life is, some version of reality will always come to get you, let no one tell you otherwise—I was at a wedding reception when I met a woman who appeared vaguely familiar. When I told her my name she laughed and said she knew something she bet I didn't know: "You fired my niece twenty years ago."

This particular woman was about my age, heavy-set, sloppily drunk, and extremely talkative. She was laughing as she spoke. She looked, I could see now, a lot like Paula and her brother. And apparently she knew my name because I was a family legend of some sort.

I found out from that woman what I could about Paula's life.

Paula—get ready for this—is a chief executive officer of a major marketing company. I felt disoriented for a moment. Who could have predicted it? Paula must fire people all the time. You can't be in a position like that without ruining people's lives. Paula, I learned, was also married and the mother of a teenage daughter. A powerful person. Our Paula.

But I didn't think I would drop Paula a line of congratulations for her good fortune and hard work even if her family laughed about her first job now. I knew what it had cost her.

"Don't feel bad about firing her," Paula's aunt said, looking right into my eyes. "It was nothing to her. It was amusing. Given everything she had to deal with it was nothing."

I was sure then that Paula must have made the firing incident into a family joke. She was fired from her first job, but look at her now.

"What about your nephew—Paula's brother?" I asked the woman. Truth be told, I had wanted to ask her about him as soon as I knew she was his aunt. I had thought of him for years really. I had even tried to imagine having someone like Paula's brother to comfort me on the two occasions when I got fired.

The wedding reception was virtually over. People were getting their coats. The roads were likely to be icy, and there was a sense of urgency in the air amid all the white and silver wedding decorations.

"What about your nephew—Paula's brother?" I asked again.

"Oh dear," the woman said. "You didn't know? Paula doesn't have a brother. You must mean Michael." She paused and then I felt her determination—she would be swift, and she would lower her voice so we would have our privacy.

"I don't like to speak ill of Michael, but he enjoyed fooling people. Paula didn't like to do that, but he liked to go around pretending they were brother and sister."

She must have registered the look on my face because she went on speaking even more quickly. "I know. I know," she said. "It was strange. He liked to call Paula his sister. It was his strange joke—a kind of compulsion. He did it even in front of me. But I shouldn't talk ill of the dead."

"What?"

"I'm surprised you didn't know. Hodgkin's disease. He must have been fighting it when Paula worked for you. I thought everybody knew. I thought you knew. You hired his sister."

"But Paula—."

"Lynn was his sister's name, I think. No, Linda. Linda was his actual sister."

I was swimming in confusion. "The only person I ever fired in my entire life was Paula," I said, "and I shouldn't have."

In my mind's eye I saw Linda with all those knitting needles hanging over her head, and I felt what people used to call Holy Fear, the fear of a jealous God's revenge.

Already I have had a long life, filled to the hilt with mistakes, but I'll say this: it is a terrible perversion to harm the living just because you want to injure the dying.

It's not that I'm bragging about, at last, knowing what I know. Or pretending in some mealy-mouthed way that I should have known more than I knew years ago. He took my breath away, I used to think of the beautiful young man who said he was Paula's brother.

Why wouldn't I have believed whatever he said: the man I thought was Paula's brother? If I had known the truth I wouldn't have said anything anyway. That's what beauty and politeness do. When you see those two possibilities together in one person that person can lie to your face. You don't say: Your real sister believes she's the love of your life, not Paula. And you play your little game with Paula because your sister is right. You let Paula go, I didn't. Would I have said that? It's only family members who can correct one another that thoroughly and ruin each other in the process. Like anyone, even the bravest of the lot, it's cowardice I understand.

The Live One

On the morning that Clint Pouvretz left for the retreat, Tesia's face was half-buried in blankets in their overly air-conditioned bedroom. She struggled with her pillow and whispered what sounded like, "Be careful." He was reasonably sure she understood he was leaving for days, which filled him with a sensation hard to bear. He loved—it was beyond love—her imitation of the superintendent of schools, her conspiracy theories about zoning boards, her dedication to the troubled children in her art classes. He couldn't be grateful enough about having all that intelligence lying next to him almost every night and about watching her nearly every morning as she leaned over and kissed him goodbye, even those times when her satchel slid off her shoulder and she cracked him in the skull with the holster of her glue gun.

That she had been relentlessly unfaithful to him—falling in love every few months with one man after another—was something he would never get used to. Although it was something he had—somehow—to endure. Her father had left the family when she was a kid and that explained a lot. It was hard for her to trust. So if he hung tough throughout all this—all these humiliations, not to mention the way his stomach felt like it had been scraped out, and his throat too, and lately there was this tornado in his head—if he could endure what was happening she would soon enough understand that he wasn't like her father. He wasn't even remotely like the kind of man who would abandon a woman. No matter what she did.

"Handshake's a little rough for you?" The staff member wore a name tag over his black T-shirt that read "Oscar." He tucked his chin into his neck, an effect that made his laugh sound like throat-clearing. His nostrils, rimmed with red spider veins, widened. The obvious occurred to Clint. Unsettlingly enough, Oscar was smelling him.

"When we're finished with you," Oscar said, "you'll be more aware of your own strength than you are of mine."

Already Clint knew his head must glow more than those paper lanterns that used to float on wires at spring sales promotions.

Two hours later, Clint stood at the end of a line of men on a stage, waiting for a snake to crawl to his outstretched arms. A minute ago a camp staffer had come onstage wearing the snake around his waist like the belt to a bathrobe. Now the staffer was handing the snake to the main speaker who was trying to make a point while the snake waved its head around like a self-conscious drunk.

So what, Clint told himself. A snake.

A snake. Only one.

But it was the color of creamed corn.

Out of the corner of his eye Clint watched as the retreat's main speaker stood up from his chair, his back erect, as if braced. He was an older man, and like Oscar he appeared certain of himself in a way that made Clint sick to his stomach. The speaker held up the snake and said, "If you believe God cut off Satan's legs to make this—if you think this creature—unique in its separateness—has nothing to teach you, you've defiled yourself."

The speaker suspended the snake like pulled taffy over the first man in line. Immediately, the snake began sucking itself along the man's arm. Its skin looked like it should snag.

Inside his left ear Clint's heart fluttered. His skin prickled as if every hair was standing. The snake aimed for him. The head and the first inches of the snake seemed separate from the rest of the snake, like that part of the snake was on a pulley. Clint could see only one eye of the snake, a wet dark thing right near the hidden mouth. The snake swiveled against his elbow and then across his forearm and the sensation was odd, almost like a kiss, a horrible kiss.

The retreat's main speaker addressed Clint with what sounded like hate: "If you don't want to experience snakebite you're going to have to relax." The speaker turned to the audience and raised his voice. "And don't think you're not somebody's snake. Because you are. Somebody's snake. Some tongue-flicking reptile to somebody. But you know what? You don't have to impress your enemy. He doesn't matter to you. Because you've got coverage."

A familiar voice muttered from the audience. It sounded like the voice was saying, "I can't see." It had to be Norman, Clint's cabinmate. Guys like Norman used to be in TV ads: good-looking men—before advertisers found out that people were more comfortable viewing soft chinless men with obvious medical conditions. A face like Norman's could only have a future in print ads. More voices erupted from the audience.

"I bet it feels like cool butter."

"I can't believe it's not butter."

The voices—they helped. Say more stupid things, Clint wanted to beg. Say stupid things so I don't have to live in my own mind right now.

And then, as if mercy rained upon Clint, an attendant directed the snake with a stick, making it muscle-glide over to another man. Clint knew that the snake could wriggle toward him again, but there were men onstage who looked even more miserable than he was and thus would prove more attractive. He imagined that he heard knees knocking. Could that be possible?

"If you learn to comprehend exactly what you fear—if and only if—you'll be able to look at anything without turning away. You will face the truth. You will triumph over life's many tests. And then—through your example—you can be a misery to your enemies even after you're dead. More people suffer snakebite from handling a dead snake than from handling a live one.

"Intuition. It's not a word you've probably thought of in terms of yourself. It's a word you should steal back. There was a time when great hunting parties crossed over these passes. There was a time when men such as yourselves lived off the natural world without the constant streams of communication that are meant to confuse you. You came here because you heeded a call. That instigation—whoever or whatever told you it's your time to arrive here—that instigation was one you could have ignored or resisted. But no. You wanted to change your life."

Clint told himself: pity the snake. Poor snake. Poor confused bitch of a snake.

After Clint galloped off the stage and collapsed on a chair, Norman said, "This was all carefully planned to be enormously cheap." He stroked his own arm as if testing it for durability. "Everything that guy said was contradictory. Although one thing's true: that thing he said about snakes biting after they're dead. So you were safe up there, given that the snake was alive. It's a reflex maybe?"

After dinner Clint and Norman weren't ten yards from the door of their cabin when the sound of huffing began. A string of shredding noises erupted, followed by crackling. At the cabin door Clint turned but couldn't make out anything except shadows and a flash of white.

"Raccoons?" Norman asked in a half-whisper. "They can be rabid."

Norman flopped onto his cot while Clint stood by the window to see if he could detect whatever was making the racket. Within seconds everything was quiet again. In the purple half-illuminated darkness beyond the window he could see a young birch, ill-nourished, struggling, between two elderberry bushes. Whatever had been tearing around in the camp must have disappeared.

He wondered if he should disappear too. He knew that he was in an alternate world—a place that no doubt over the years many campers had yearned to be rescued from. He wondered if every cabin held the memory of countless dank afternoons when puzzles shed crucial pieces. Of course not only children had used the camp. Religious groups? More likely hunters, roughing it with bottles of Smirnoff rolling over the floorboards.

While he was fumbling around he found an old dirty round thing in a crevice of the rickety box that served as his nightstand. He opened the lid. Inside, a plastic girl revolved in a plastic room. A tiny plastic couch was pushed up against a tiny wall. He closed the compact and read the inscription: Polly Pocket. Evidently a Girl Scout troop or some other little girl group had used the cabin. And left behind Polly Pocket, destined to turn in a circle forever. More like Pocket Neurotic. The limited view, the repetitive lifestyle, the claustrophobia. The ugly thought: no wonder Tesia wanted to leave him.

He turned off the light and lay on his cot.

In the dark Norman's face gave off a shine like cellophane. "You were supposed to bring a pillow," he said. "It was on the website."

"Developing strength. The first step."

The silence in the cabin grew thick. Norman broke it. "Do you believe in the existence of ghosts?"

"I'm kind of an agnostic about that."

"I don't want to believe in them—but I've had experiences with them. They're clots. Clots of perception. Not clots of feeling. Places where too much was experienced. Filled-up spaces that ought to be drained. They're clouds basically."

"I thought they were clots."

"Clots and clouds."

"You see ghosts?"

"I go somewhere, and it's like there's a catch in the air. Everything slows down. They want to touch me."

Oh no. Here we go.

"The first time was in an old bed and breakfast. The hotels were all filled, and so I was stuck. Uncomfortable antique furniture. Ghosts rustling around, crashing into things. Like what we heard outside tonight. Ghosts are restless. They're restless because they don't have a relationship with their bodies anymore. Are you capable of understanding that? A lot of people aren't capable of understanding that. Ghosts aren't bodies. They're desperate to touch another body. To inhabit a body."

"Do you mean they're parasites?"

"They'd like to be," Norman said. "That's their ambition. Their particular challenge, given their memories of their physical selves. I hope you know that what I'm talking about is the real deal. The real real deal." For a moment Clint thought his cabinmate was referring to his own body.

Norman wasn't finished. "You think I'm gullible. Everyone's gullible in their own way. Their own provincial way. Have you ever contacted a psychic on-line? It's a flatter-and-scare sandwich. She tells you that you must be brilliant, possibly you're a psychic yourself, and that the next seventy-two days will see the transit of Saturn. I know what's going on with fakes. I'm intrigued, but I'm not gullible."

Norman reminded Clint of a guy he knew back in high school whose greatest desire was to be the football mascot. That guy wore a big orange bird costume that looked like a fuzzy wrecking ball. He was honored to wear that big stinking costume.

Norman was saying, "That's why I've decided that overall I like this retreat. It's not fake. It's the genuine thing. No big promises. Not once were we told what the future holds. You don't believe me about the ghosts."

"I guess I don't know enough about ghosts."

"The thing about ghosts that you should know: they want to be recognized. People talk about a clammy feeling from ghosts. That's cold energy the ghosts are gathering, and it's from us. Our clamminess. They're the ones who want to be shocked. They eat fear. Being afraid is close to being alive so they try to frighten themselves as much as us."

"Do you actually think what we heard tonight—."

"I'm going to say it was an animal. But it was a reminder too. I've felt that same energy before. Powerful forces are at work."

Clint couldn't help himself. "Weak ones too," he said.

Lee Upton

As Clint pretended to be asleep gnawing erupted above him. It sounded like he was inside a living thing, inside a stomach maybe, even though the sound must be coming from some small roof-dwelling mammal. To focus his mind, he made himself remember the early days with Tesia. One particular thing—the childhood incident she told him about—that was something he never figured out.

Tesia had complained that a memory came to her in flashes. Or was it a dream, a remembered dream that crossed over to resemble reality? Did he really want to hear this? Of course. Come on, Tesia.

She would have been about five years old, which accounted for why the memory was unreliable. Her father had left the family about a year before then. Her sister Becky's boyfriend, the kind of boy who made a habit of running around graveyards, showed up while Tesia was being babysat by Becky. Clint could imagine that boy—a thick-shouldered bully always saying, "Don't you trust me?" True to form, the boy got Becky and Tesia to go with him to an abandoned house. And then—this is awful: Tesia, a little child, was left alone in a room of that house. What she remembers: the vastness of the room. As her eyes grew accustomed to the dark, objects materialized: dressers, a sheeted crib, chairs. The dust was peculiar. "It was like overly aged dust. But isn't it odd to think such a thing? Do five-year-olds think like that?" As she spoke, Clint noticed what had escaped his attention—the gold rifts in Tesia's eyes. Her eyes had tiny rays in them, as if they had been sliced. Her beautiful and disconcerting uniqueness was alive to him.

Dust, Tesia was saying, dust was what she was sure of. Throat-clogging dust. She was upstairs in the abandoned house, alone and terrified. She was just a little girl, and in the dark her bare legs gave off a funny silky light. The moon must have come out from a cloud because there was silver at the edge of the window shade. When she turned from looking at the window, her head swimming with the deep tiredness that only children know, she saw movement. Tugging. Something was moving underneath a dresser. Tugging. Tugging. Tugging. Poking out from behind a stack of boards was a child's leg.

The next thing she remembers: she is screaming, and her sister Becky is again with her, and the two of them are running down the stairs.

Clint couldn't wait to do the obvious. He asked for Becky's number, pulled out his cell phone and called her. Becky picked up, tried to remember the incident, kept failing and then, finally, it was coming back. Oh that. A practical joke. She and the boy found a doll and were hiding with it and making it move—to scare Tesia.

Lying on a cot in a cabin with a man across the room convinced of the existence of ghosts, Clint thought about how a silly trick had shattered into nightmares for Tesia. That she hadn't confronted her own sister when the memories returned seemed like timidity or stupidity, almost as if her suffering served a purpose. After talking to Becky he had hung up the phone and waited for Tesia to show her gratitude to him for solving the mystery. Instead she left him for three days. The guy turned out to be a pharmacist.

If finding the truth was not what Tesia needed, what did she need? Try as he might, he couldn't reach Tesia. A thin gummy sheet hung between them. A thin sheaf—the image of a prophylactic assailed him—thinner than shed snakeskin. He considered: was she trying to end their marriage? Poking at the marriage with a hot knife till it split?

Why did it always come for him: this sensation of being haunted by something he had forgotten or neglected to understand? As if on the road not taken there was some poor lost thing he'd left, not even recognizably human, this thing, and yet with a human soul.

On the morning before the second-to-last day of the retreat, when the other men plunged ahead on a nature walk, Clint asked Norman, "Are you really getting anything out of this?"

"What's this?" Norman asked.

"The retreat."

"I don't know anymore," Norman said. He looked less healthy today, less like a full-page ad. "I thought I was. I keep hoping. Kind of desperately. But then again I get stuff out of everything. I get stuff out of you. Just watching you. Stuff I don't need to get, but it's still stuff."

Clint considered. "If you can get stuff out of anything and anyone—why did you come here? Why pay for stuff you can get anywhere?"

"Are you trying to insult me?"

"No. It's an authentic question."

"It's fine with me if you're trying to insult me."

"I'm not, not even if you get stuff out of being insulted."

"I guess I do like the idea of strength—developing it," Norman said. "It's not something I'm known for. It's flexibility I'm known for. And besides it's actual, you know, not wired. Or wireless. I guess it's wireless. But actual. Actual people. Actual trees. Actual birds. It's like things are happening right in front of me. It's not—you know—spectral. Sorry for wigging you out about the ghosts. But, you know, you're hard to talk to. It's like you short-circuit things. You don't hear. It's

Lee Upton

[104]

like talking into a microphone and then the microphone goes dead, you know?"

It was a dream of water, a perfect inset of water: like the sky had been liquefied and a corner of paradise fell to earth. Why enter such a pond? It would be enough just to look.

"This might be bottomless," Norman said, "like a quarry. A good place to get rid of things. I mean you go in there and it's like you're in a stew of you don't know what."

Most of the men from the camp were already there. But no one was going in. Or unbuckling.

Then a man who looked like a Viking—his knees were the size of colanders—strode down the bank, pulling off his shirt. At the pond's edge he hesitated, took three giant steps, and disappeared under the water. When he came up, his hair streaming over his forehead, he was smiling.

"How is it?" Norman yelled. He danced around, trying to get out of his shorts.

Without answering, the Viking plunged under the water again.

Clint wrapped his glasses in his shirt and set the bundle on a rock. Instantly the men around him were reduced to fuzzy grayness. Once in the pond he let himself fall face forward. Even without his glasses he could see what looked like a thicket far underwater, magnified, as if a forest were flooded below him. He bobbed upright and floated on his back, the sun beating against his forehead.

Norman's voice was echoing in his ear. "Buzzards are circling overhead. Do you think that means we're supper?"

Clint couldn't see anything.

"Maybe they prefer dead meat." It was still Norman's voice.

Lee Upton

The voice sounded like it was bobbing.

Clint played with the idea that he was floating in anesthetic instead of a mountain cavity filled by an underground spring. He swam away from the body that was likely to belong to Norman.

It wasn't long afterwards that a wall of silver erupted like a flash bulb. Jets of spray flew into Clint's eyes. The pond was being tilted. He rotated with all his strength and swam to shore where he hobbled to find his glasses, wiping them on his unrolled shirt.

He turned just as the Viking with the huge knees was setting a body on the bank, laying it down like carpeting. It was Norman.

Norman's lungs were fine—given that he was shouting. At first Clint couldn't make out the words and then he wished he hadn't. "You wanted it," Norman shouted. "You let it happen. You know I'm talking to you. It would've been perfect for you if I drowned. Afraid I'd pull you down."

Was Norman talking to him? Was that what the splashing had been about? Was Clint being accused of nearly letting Norman drown?

The other men dropped their eyes as Clint searched one face after another. Then Clint backed up and returned with Norman's clothes, knelt, and handed the bundle over.

Norman wobbled upright, tried to get into the legs of his shorts, and began a little hopping sequence that dispersed the crowd.

"I'd never want to see you drowned," Clint said. He took off his glasses and rubbed away the smear that was making everything look sugared. He put his glasses back on.

"So you never want to see me drowned?" Norman said.

"That's rich. You don't want to be a witness, that's all."

Clint mused on how much he hated the expression *That's rich.*

Norman wasn't finished. "You didn't do anything to stop it."

An unassailable belief of Clint's: he would not willingly or consciously contribute to anyone's suffering for as long as he lived.

The last thing Clint wanted: to return to the camp. He walked in the opposite direction of the other retreaters. Within a hundred yards, three paths converged. He took the widest. Thick with pine needles, the path died in bracken before opening out again. A rush of heat swept across his face. He set off between firs until he found another path, this one narrower.

He was entirely alone. Which meant he could think—undisturbed—about his life. In other words, Tesia.

He didn't understand the sort of men who blew their wives away with a shotgun. He did understand stalking. Being married to Tesia—it was like stalking in slow motion. He would never leave her. She knew that. It was like the men who came for her knew that too. Which gave him hope. She'd grow out of it. Or she'd grow older. And this crazy desperate horror show would stop. They had an unspoken agreement. If he could endure the wait. He had to remind himself: those men weren't giving her what she really wanted. Although neither was he. Obviously she didn't know what she wanted. She didn't understand herself. She liked to terrorize herself as much as she liked to terrorize him.

He must have been walking for at least another half hour before the path nearly disappeared again. Piles of logs were spattered with bomb craters of lichen. More brambles blocked his way. He thought that he might be approaching, from the opposite side, the berry patch he and the other men visited earlier in the week. He smelled ash from the dead ring of a campfire. Further ahead a circle of yellow grass looked burned by a giant magnifying glass. To his left, more brambles in bundles. A briar snagged at his shirt, dragged at his arm, and broke the skin. He tripped on, before stopping to clean the steam off his glasses with his shirt.

Past a stand of birches he caught sight of a pond that made a perfect round impression, as if a meteor stunned the mountain and for a thousand years rainwater dropped to form a silver cavity. He thought of going there, stripping off his clothes, walking in and not caring. Maybe he'd float. Maybe he wouldn't.

All he knew: it was a good thing—to be alone. A good thing. Although he couldn't get himself to think full thoughts for more than a minute. For now, it was enough to experience the hot wind, to listen for the sounds of rushing water somewhere up ahead.

The hair rose on his neck. A heap of something. Off the path.

He shivered, thinking he was seeing a rubber prop. Instead it was skin. A human body, a body like a pelt—flattened and naked, with dark nipples. Brambles were piled against the body and more brush. He found himself moving forward and bending over the woman, despite his terror. He made his palm graze the body's bare stomach. Under his hand: soft heat.

He pawed around the ground and found nothing to cover her. She must have been dragged here after her clothes were stripped. He took off his shirt and pressed it across the woman. He hoisted her body into his arms, her head hanging over his elbow, her neck exposed, her abdomen crumbled up against him. His wadded shirt fell off her. Whoever had done this might come back. Or an animal could find the body.

He was running with the woman in his arms, stopping when his knees gave. She was slippery and her head wobbled. He tucked his neck in and saw that a bruise had spread to her ear. He stopped again, drawing up his knee to push her higher and fold her against his chest. He listened for the sound of water, but no, it was traffic, an engine heading over the rise.

He ran hard until he was in a ditch, splashing through water, and then stumbling out, nearly dropping the woman, nearly letting her body graze the ground again.

Then he was on the side of a road and then in the middle of the road and shouting and not knowing if whoever was in the truck on that isolated stretch of gravel might be a killer or someone innocent who would stop and save the woman.

The sweat in his eyes and on the lenses of his glasses kept him from seeing whoever was in the truck racing toward him while he held the naked woman in his arms. As he held her out—she was heavier by the second and sliding again—it flashed through his mind that the sight must be terrifying, as if he was offering a sacrifice to the world, as if he wanted to offer this vulnerable body to anyone in the world who passed, when the truth was—even for a stranger—he would sacrifice himself first.

As the truck barreled toward him he closed his eyes from the dust and felt, he could not then know why, a terrible sense of power. The sensation was familiar. It was just that never before had he known it to be power.

You Know You've Made It When They Hate You

Moi and The King: Charity
Performance Nearly Worth the Ticket

Last night's opening of *The King & I*, in which
costume design trumped character, turned the tables on the painful posing of the original, revealing
the sodden colonial politics underpinning the tired
enterprise, from the remarkable hoop skirt of Anna
to the exciting cummerbund of her countryman.
Molly Crane as Anna overwhelmed the role until
this reviewer wondered if the production shouldn't
have been called *Moi & the King*. She was in medi-
ocre vocal frame and bent on too heavy-handedly
stirring the sexual waters between herself and the
polygamous Siamese monarch. Generally her role
is played with some subtlety and a dose of British
rectitude. Or what the British want us to suppose is
rectitude. Here we have an Anna salivating for her
king and ready to flash her knickers every time she
executes a turn-about in her hoop skirt, marvel-
ously designed by Mary Achtenberg with delicate
hand-embroidered detailing.

The King—one of the newest Korean neighbors
in our venerable burg—acquitted himself with
dignity in the midst of Anna's incessant bosom-
beating innuendoes of sexual congress. One could
see that he felt oppressed by the shrewishly seductive
manipulations of Anna, a widow who recklessly
inspired a romance between one of the king's
countless concubines and a shirtless youth.

The surprise of the evening was John Fostergarth,
whose hapless portrayal sent laughter to all corners,

once the audience realized the joke: the representative of British imperialism was staggeringly at odds with himself and his position. Fostergarth's mimicry of stage fright propelled gales of mirth throughout the otherwise often puzzled audience. His reedy figure, excellently attired in evening clothes of a fit and condition rarely seen locally, slowly became saturated with the self-consuming perspiration of the colonialist frustrated by his own unruly instincts. As with his compatriot Anna, we were led to intuit the venality beneath the skin of civility. Given secrecy and opportunity, the hoop skirt and the dinner jacket are flung aside as impulses from the gutter fly.

Such an unpeeling of the mendacities of xenophobia is nearly worth the price of admission for this chestnut, with musical direction by Timothy Flock. Superb costumes by Mary Achtenberg. . . .

Shampoo, Please!

Can someone wash this musical right out of our hair? We know its message: its flagrant attempt to naturalize the desire of an empire attempting to control far distant real estate, the despoiling and the selling of our own special islands. But what's *South Pacific* without manic dancing by unrepentant youths? We know the boar's tooth ceremony is a big crowd-pleaser. But call me a cock-eyed pessimist, the mature killer, the mysterious Frenchman in this hare-brained production, is younger than Nellie Forbush, who simply sounds developmentally delayed. The tired, pinched-looking star behind this vehicle is Molly Crane. Are we to find xenophobia charming? No naïve waif is she from Little Rock. Her doubling up preposterously as Bloody Mary might have worked if the audience hadn't been baffled into submission.

John Fostergarth fills the bill as Stew Pot, swallowing the role whole and belching up a more-than-competent performance in what is otherwise a carnival of incompetence—except for costume design, by the delightful and talented. . . .

My Fat Friar

The rain in Spain falls mainly on this musical. With a lil bit of luck you'll miss it. Molly Crane as Eliza Doolittle hardens the heart and then some. Impossible to believe a transformation will take place from filthy flower peddler to stately avatar of elitism. Wilfred Oneff as Henry Higgins takes on a preposterous role with aplomb, despite his sorry voice.

John Fostergarth, still quite new to the stage but certain to be a favorite, pours on the charm as an idle dandy at the horse track.

Molly Crane almost comes to life when she warbles "I Could Have Danced All Night." Here we believe her—and see shining beneath the grease paint a glimmer of what might have been. A tiny ray of sunlight in a chilly production.

Unfortunately, you can't change a tramp into a delicacy, especially one with a backwoods accent. Who wants to see a lady clacking about onstage in a sheath with ropelike sash? In early scenes we might be tempted to call the play *My Fat Friar*. But costume is necessary to suggest the tawdry Doolittle's class-jumping aspirations. . . .

❖ ❖ ❖

Why should Roger Dillingham, the reviewer for *The Pattwell Gazette*, despise Molly Crane? For despise her he did: her artificial gestures, overinflated, unforgettable. Once, halfway through *Oklahoma!*, he snuck a detective novel out of his raincoat and began reading by penlight until she came back onstage—her hair stacked on her head so idiotically that he couldn't concentrate on his novel again. Of course she performed without any sense of irony. Of course she floated onstage like a helium-inflated troll.

For at least five musicals and two farces he had reviewed her and suffered.

It was queasy-making just to watch her. No matter where Roger Dillingham sat in the theater, she seemed close to him, and intimate with him, and he felt manipulated. Afterwards, when he got back to his apartment and fired up his word processor, he atomized her faults until the fug dissipated.

Why couldn't the theater ever put on a meaningful production for charity—something on the order of *Mother Courage*, or a stage version of *The Battle of Algiers*?

It was no wonder that Roger Dillingham felt compelled to praise John Fostergarth. The rumor was that Fostergarth vomited in a towel before performances. He was the perfect foil for Molly Crane. He was far worse than she could ever be. And the costume designer, the abominable Mary Achtenberg. Well, if Roger Dillingham didn't praise anything in the production his editor would think he was being unfair.

Roger Dillingham rested on a chaise lounge, his legs stretched out before him while the turquoise waters of the swimming pool ricocheted light. When he looked up from his novel, he saw Molly Crane.

A boy with a beach ball walked behind her and she swiveled. Why was she here at the Circle of Health in her yellow swimsuit, her hair flattened on the back of her head like a pancake?

Roger himself wouldn't be here if he hadn't been hoodwinked by his aged parents, who agreed to donate to three charities an amount equal to that of a ten-day stay at the Circle of Health. Given that Roger had so little money and was proud of it, they paid for his airfare too. His mother came to his apartment and stepped over the tottering cascades of charity brochures. She stood before him in a gypsy peasant dress, a thick, bullish old woman whose long-practiced aversion to anything but her family's physical comfort and aesthetic enjoyment stunned him. Rather than agree to donate out of the goodness of her heart to any number of worthy causes, she struck a deal. "You yourself are a worthwhile cause," she said. "You yourself are a charity case." She and his father were perfectly content to plunge all their energy into interior decoration, long-term upscaling of the arboretum, and the mass-marketing of bonsai. Roger could never make up for his parents' profligate ways, their studious avoidance of reality. They were the products of their own fantasies. They would never let him ignore them. They were two elderly cases of arrested development. And now here he was, sunk in a hub of self-infatuation, of fatuous over-indulgence: a health complex.

But why should Molly Crane be at a health resort, her legs thicker at the thighs than he expected, laid out on her own chaise lounge? Why should she need to restore her undeniably good health? She could bounce through five matinées and four supper shows a week.

Roger twisted about to get a better view of her, just as her own head snapped around and he was caught staring. Her bangs were plastered to her forehead like a Roman centurion's. Her eyes were almost purple, as if dipped in some strange planetary gas. She knew him. He knew she recognized him. He ducked.

Lee Upton

Someone must have pointed Roger out to her one night at the theater, and now she had at least two choices: snub him or confront him. She reached into her straw bag and drew out her sunglasses, swung her legs over the side of her chaise lounge, grabbed her straw bag, and slung her towel over her arm. He had seen her enough in the theater to know she was about to call out to him. There it was: that grim thrust to her jaw. Her broad mouth opened slightly, gasping with concentration.

Oh God save me, Roger nearly cried aloud. But he could thank his stars: she had a knot of teenagers to make her way around before she could reach him. Roger didn't even bother to pick up his detective novel. He rose, and then, with deep embarrassment, for he hated the thought of Molly Crane seeing him in his swimming trunks, he turned and fled. He could imagine what he looked like to her from behind: the landslide of his backside muscles.

He wound his way between metal tables and nearly tripped over one whining toddler as the walkway curved. He passed a stretch of bungalows and a patch of young women who stared at him unselfconsciously.

He knew Molly Crane's type: she wanted to get him alone, out among the banana palms, and give him a very loud piece of her mind.

His chest felt ready to explode, but his hotel room was well beyond the gift shop, and he doubted he could keep up his pace and make it to his room. When his breathing grew even more labored, he paused and looked back. At least twenty yards separated him from her, but she was still heading toward him, the black ovals of her sunglasses glinting.

A couple in swimsuits and thongs blocked his way. What now? A tiki shed rose to his right, unoccupied. Fronds crisscrossed near him in a Polynesian tableau.

He was practically running when, suddenly, he was sure he was alone. He couldn't see Molly Crane in any direction. He had come full circle, back to the gate of the pool.

Once more he stretched out on the same chaise lounge he had vacated. He picked up his detective novel. He couldn't remember who the victim was, but the top of his head and his arms were burning, and his breathing wasn't yet under control, and he was staring into the pages of his book trying to make the words stay still when she sat next to him, lowering herself into a chaise lounge.

Molly Crane shifted her weight and took off her sunglasses, and it occurred to Roger that she no longer intended to speak to him but to bully him with her gummy physical presence, her thick thighs and long calves and tiny ankles where he thought—the sweat kept running into his eyes—he could see a pulsebeat. She made his own body look like a burst sausage, like a big useless sack that he was stuck in. He despised himself for hating his body, for allowing himself to feel any concern for his body when there were so many more important things to think about in the world. Virtually anything. Anything was more important.

When he could look up, Roger saw that a couple were stirring themselves into the whirlpool near the tiki shed. Even Molly Crane wouldn't follow him into the close orbit of a pair of lovers in a hot tub. She wouldn't go to such a length. She couldn't berate him over the noise of the spray jets. A woman like that demanded to be heard.

And, anyway, if he could catch his breath maybe he would be the one Molly Crane should worry about. Maybe he would be the one to start shouting. Maybe she would be the one to be terrorized. Maybe she would be the one who was afraid to be torn apart. He could eviscerate her and pull out her voice box and send all her bodily organs floating in the whirlpool like so much dim sum. He could show her what this world is all about. Because, Molly Crane, I want you to know it's not made of musical romances for unhinged women—and then, his breath catching, he vividly recalled watching her sing onstage, full-throated, her dreamy eyes gazing upward. What was she so emotional about? She was singing "Hello, Young Lovers" to a plank of plywood in the upper balcony.

Molly Crane was sure it was him. Dang! She was practically jogging to keep him in sight after she discovered him at the swimming pool. She had thought she lost him for a while there. But then she was smart enough to work her way around the pool past the white metal tables with their giant umbrellas, and she trotted right up to his chaise lounge, right up close to him, letting her shadow fall onto his paperback.

Maybe she had only imagined that he was running away. He might not even know who she is—looking like this, out of stage makeup and no longer in one of those ridiculous wigs that Mary kept insisting she wear.

She couldn't believe it: Roger Dillingham. Dang!

Here was the man who made her want to crawl and die after every opening night at the playhouse. Yes. Roger Dillingham, the man John referred to as the MOB—Mean Old Bastard.

If only she could get Roger Dillingham to stop being so harsh. His harshness was inhibiting everyone—Neddy, Alfred, Germaine, Christopher, Margaret, Barney Kim, John. They were all depressed. Poor John took it hardest. By the end of any opening night he was throwing up air. And John had been through so much. He was the best brother in the world, the sweetest, the kindest. Their father used to joke: any closer and you'd be twins.

But why was Roger Dillingham standing up now? Stay, she wanted to beg him. Stay. If she could only get up the nerve to talk to him, really talk to him, and convince him how hard she tried. She was even going to be taking lessons in Macon from a woman who had worked on two soap operas. You can be put through nearly every emotion in a soap opera: all those funerals and weddings and kidnappings and electrocutions and courts of law. And Molly was going to try so hard to learn how to act. She was. She was the first to admit she couldn't imagine what she was good at on the stage—unless it was playing a woman older than herself. She was twenty-three years old and Roger Dillingham kept writing about her as if she were ancient. But she had gone through things, so he must be intuitive. She was a widow, after all. Even if she wasn't good at being a widow. She hardly had begun to love her husband enough—but that was because John was so much in the way. There. She admitted it. John was in the way.

She watched, stiffening with anxiety, as Roger Dillingham padded off—until she saw that he was aiming for the whirlpool. So. He wasn't avoiding her after all. The back of his head gleamed above the pool's rim.

In the name of her brother John, in the name of poor wonderful John, Molly Crane dropped her towel and sprinted after Roger Dillingham. Any musical is no more believable than the contents of a snow globe, she told herself, but you have to believe, you have to give your spirit to it. And she couldn't help but want better things for the playhouse, and for John. She imagined that Roger Dillingham's eyes would harden with dislike if he recognized her. But surely this was because he couldn't see into her heart.

A nice-looking couple were vacating the pool when Molly began to lower herself just two jets away from her reviewer on his side of the curve.

Dang! Infernal whirlpool heat! My loving God! Dang!

Molly breathed steam into her lungs. What if her skin slid off her bones like a boiled chicken's?

All right. She would live.

And couldn't the heat stimulate a conversation? Surely she could start a conversation with Roger Dillingham about the heat. She could say: Excuse me, do you believe you have any skin that's not parboiled? The suction too—the suction. She had heard of people sucked to the bottom of whirlpools. Years ago someone had warned her: Never duck your head under the water. She could start up a conversation about the suction. She couldn't help but imagine John's comment if he were here: You can tell Roger Dillingham he really sucks.

She took another breath, and another and another, and then the heat didn't feel bad at all. She closed her eyes and leaned backward and felt the sun play against her eyelids. She had a little time to get up her courage. Roger Dillingham wouldn't have submerged himself up to his neck if he didn't intend to stay and get a good soaking. A good soaking could only blanch out bad feelings, and Molly hoped a good soaking would leach away her own faults: my pettiness, she thought, my resentment, my small-mindedness. God, make me your vessel.

She trained her eyes away from his. It was worse than being in an elevator. You couldn't let your eyes linger. You looked up or out to a tiny point just lower in space than a man's armpit.

Otherwise your eyes were violating him. You held yourself back as a courtesy. At most you might make a comment about the weather—language that meant, We won't harm each other. John. John sometimes used an old expression of their mother's: "Don't worry. They can't eat me." Not that John believed such wisdom.

It would take a little longer and she would loosen up, that was all, and start a conversation. She didn't have to accost Roger Dillingham at once. She didn't have to give him the impression that she was stalking him. She could make it look as if the realization of his identity came upon her slowly, here in the churning waters under a burning sun. The recognition shouldn't appear *forced*. She knew her face was as wet as a seal's and flushed, and that even if she introduced herself, it would take him a minute to connect the name with the face.

How bad could Roger Dillingham be? He liked John after all. In his reviews he was always praising John more than anyone else, except for Mary. That was because he understood how remarkable John was. When not even three specialists could figure out what was wrong with John—that's when John wanted to act at the playhouse. And who could say no to him? Everyone thought he was dying—all through *My Fair Lady*, all through *South Pacific*, all through *A Funny Thing Happened on the Way to the Forum*. But then right during the second week of *The Fantasticks* there was the miraculous transformation. But even then he was still dependent on her, afraid of every little thing and of everyone but her. And then he invested his entire inheritance from their parents into the playhouse.

"You know you've made it when they hate you," John said about the reviews. But if Molly could get some constructive criticism, if she could find out why she was held in contempt by Roger Dillingham, the only person who ever reviewed community theater in the county . . .

Although she feared his answer: she wasn't convincing as a woman falling in love. And she knew why: she couldn't love—not in the normal way. She couldn't initiate the emotional progression. John didn't die, but her husband did, and she wasn't there for him. She hadn't been there for him or seen his death and hadn't begun to love him maturely, no, and now she could never love again. Except for John, who was at this hour up in their room napping, because he was so skinny, and he needed so much rest before he met with the acupuncturist. And somehow she was sure Roger Dillingham sensed how distanced she was from mature love, from the desires of the women she impersonated. And she worried now that her own love for John was harmful. It kept John from a real life, so that he was a dandy at the racetrack or an ambassador of the British empire every weekend when he could be finding someone to love him now that it looked like he was going to live a lot longer. You can't stop people from wanting love. And Molly knew she had hardly brought her love to bear before Anthony left the house and got into their car and never came back again and then there was his body at the funeral parlor. Unrecognizable because of the accident. Like a dummy body.

She and Anthony had been kids in some ways. Married for less than a year. What she had to give Anthony had only begun to chirp inside her. It was nothing compared to what she would have given him if they had been together for even one more year. Because it takes time, because it's a risk to love someone so much, it's a discipline, and she was weak. She was as miserable at being a wife as she was at being an actress. She was only now beginning to have the heart to admit it, almost to relax into the horrible truth.

John, she thought suddenly, John could learn to relax more too. "You're so anxious," she said to him only this morning right before they checked into the resort. "But anxiety's so funny," he said.

She knows that John doesn't feel like an alien at the resort—already she knows this. She felt a change in him even as they waited for their luggage. He complained about being tired. That was to be expected, but there was something else, some flicker of withheld excitement mixed in with his anxiety. She would have to steel herself against the pressure he would put on her to change her life again for him. He couldn't imagine her outside his life anymore. Even though they both were young. Young and stunted, she thought.

A weight struck Molly Crane's neck. Roger Dillingham's head nestled into her neck, and without thinking, with only instinct to guide her, she said, "No, you can't stay, sir." His body turned heavily and his legs must have folded because he began sliding down her shoulder. She pushed at his shoulder and raised her knees to try to keep his big head from going under the water, and then she shouted and knew she was shouting loudly, more loudly than she had imagined she could before the water stung up high into her nose and the sounds of the bubbling whirlpool jets and the children' voices echoing from the swimming pool came to her distorted curiously as if everything around her was pushing her head down under the water, for here Molly was, going under with the mammoth slippery head, even while another part of her was calmly considering the situation and gathering one clear thought: Thank you, God, for my vocal training.

She lurched forward and wrapped her arms under Roger's arms, but she was sliding again and Roger was suckered onto her. The jets gushed and pulsed into her ears. She was losing her footing, and foamy water was splashing just as the lifeguard—a muscular, orange-haired woman—ran up blowing a whistle, and another lifeguard ran off blowing a whistle in the opposite direction—and Molly thought of Anna of *The King and I* who whistled a happy tune to disguise fear, and Molly thought it's no good, whistling only annoys people, only annoys people, only annoys people. But then the lifeguard was pulling Roger Dillingham off Molly Crane like he was a great big octopus. And Molly, gasping, said, "I'm okay, I'm okay." She flipped her body onto the cement and told the lifeguard—who at last drew Roger Dillingham's body onto the cement too and worked over his flesh and began flagging—"He's a good man, you can't give up, he couldn't be a better man."

The lifeguard threw her hands in the air and clenched her fists and bent to her task again, pummeling Roger Dillingham's chest with desperate new energy. She pumped at Roger's chest as if she knew he couldn't be a better man . . . as if she could save his life and with it his world, his unforgiving world that had never once satisfied him since he was a boy, never once since the days when he hadn't yet learned to read but liked to sing and do little pretend-magic tricks and even teach a dog how not to snap at a pork chop for a count of three while his mother laughed and said, "You are an imp. You are a pill. You are everything, everything, everything I ever dreamed of."

Will Anyone Ever Know Me

What did she know? What had been done to her?

The woman woke in the night and asked her husband, "Is she here?"

The man turned on the bedside light.

"She isn't here," he said.

And they felt it. Relief. An enormous relief that she wasn't in the room, that presence, that unfortunate who is not their child.

"We were selfish," she said.

"No, we did what was right."

"She's from another world. We don't even know her age."

"She's a child—whatever her age."

"We've lost everything and now this. It doesn't change that we've lost everything. I don't know if I have the strength . . . We pretended. And we stole her."

"No. Rescued."

"Stole."

"Lured her. At the worst."

"She's from so far away."

"She's who she is."

"Our daughter—our real daughter—"

"—would have wanted us to save her. It was a miracle that she wound up in our room. She's ours now."

"Ours?"

The man turned off the bedside lamp. After a while he said, "She could have Allison's room. It would be heaven for a girl like her. For any little girl."

"You don't understand how I feel—no. I won't go that far—."

"She's here." His whisper was a hiss.

In the half-darkness the woman saw the child crawling toward the edge of the bed.

"Picture for you, ma'am," the girl said.

"What, honey? Oh, honey, what?"

"For the door, ma'am. For the room."

The woman turned on the light. She looked at the picture—a stick figure of a girl with long hair.

"See. So you know."

"Did they make you put up a sign?" the woman asked.

"Yes. Yes, ma'am."

"The sign meant you were in the room and you were alone?"

"Yes."

"You don't need a sign here . . . This is a pretty picture. This is a very pretty picture. You know, you don't have to call me ma'am."

"Sorry."

"What would you like to call me?"

The child did not answer.

"Can you tell me?" the woman asked.

It was awful, everything was awful. Allison, their beloved daughter, had been lost to them. Then this other child appeared a month later when the woman was running the bathwater in the hotel and heard her husband call to her in a voice he had never used before. And there was the girl standing in the living room of their suite and it became obvious. The child had some English, enough to tell them what they needed to know, and the husband knew some of her language and so they learned more. There was no one from her family. No one left. What could the man and the woman do?

And now here she was with them—how had they done it? By what miracle could a living child be taken from one world to another, could pass through that membrane? Why had they been allowed to get away with it?

And the woman was thinking: What have we done? Will we be caught? Will it have been worth it?

It was breathtakingly easy to steal the child—and now there was no way to explain her.

The child would not sleep alone in the guest room. In the middle of the night she came into their room, night after night, to sleep on the floor near their bed. When they woke she was already looking at them. She looked as if she wasn't sure what was expected of her but that she would wait for an answer.

What did the girl know? What had been done to her?

"We did the best we could, didn't we?" the man whispered.

They could hear the child moving about in the room above their heads.

"What if they come after her?" the woman asked.

"No one will ever come after her. There are more and more and more where she came from. All those girls. They keep so many of them and use them up. She doesn't have a family. She's safe here. She's already dead to the people who forced her to go to the hotel."

"I dream about them coming for her. They take her away.

And then she's back."

"You mean—our daughter's back." In his wife's dream their daughter came back after they returned the foreign child. He knew because he had the same dream.

"It's not fair," the woman said.

The girl hardly ate and would not smile. She often looked as if she were waiting.

"She doesn't trust us."

"How could she?"

"You're right. How could she."

The woman still had Allison's passport—that was what allowed everything to happen. She had kept her daughter's passport with her, and so when the child was in their hotel suite they hardly needed to think. They knew the country was corrupt. Children could be bought. It was breathtakingly easy because their own child was not alive.

"Have you thought about giving her the room?"

"She's so strange—to give her the room—it would be like saying Allison is gone."

"Allison will never be gone. We'll never let her go. She's with us."

"Would Allison want the girl to have the room?" the woman wondered.

"She would have," the man said.

"Do you think so?"

"She was a loving girl—she would have loved to have a sister. She was a gentle girl. She shared things."

"After she turned nine. Not before. After her birthday she

started to be good about sharing with her friends. She shared some things anyway."

"She didn't share her stuffed animals. I'll admit that."

"The girl," the woman said, "—she probably would like a stuffed animal to hug at night. Maybe that's why she can't sleep. Maybe the panda family."

The woman could see them, the pandas, the mama and the papa and the baby, the two stuffed monkeys, the menagerie of tigers. The Barbies hadn't been of interest to Allison, but just the same she wound up with a lineup of them on a shelf at the headboard of her bed. Most of the dolls came from other girls who gave them to Allison at birthday parties. But the stuffed penguin—Allison wouldn't sleep without it. The stuffed penguin had been buried with Allison.

"It's all right," the man said. "I shouldn't have asked. Come on. I'm sorry. It's all right. It's all right. The guest room is nice—it's a nice room for a little girl."

What did the girl know? What had been done to her? Who would have allowed this living breathing child to stand in the middle of a strange hotel room in an adult's ruined pinkish brown evening gown torn to show her legs and with her chest nearly bare—the vulnerable breastbone standing out from her chest. The child wore a woman's high heels, heels so high and large that her foot slid into the toe, and the sole at the heel was bare. The child's eyes were rimmed with eyeliner. Trick or Treat was the woman's first thought when she walked into the living room of their suite. And then the child began to undress and the man and the woman said No No No and the child looked around wildly.

Wasn't that look there still? But even the child's fear was

somehow almost calculating. How would they ever lure her into their world?

Their own lovely daughter—the country had stolen her, the awful country that the woman had taken Allison to because the girl missed her father. They were leaving in less than two hours when the girl appeared. There was no time to waste, no time at all, and with some of the woman's clothing cut and pinned and with the child's hair washed and cut—oh, the woman was working so quickly—the child would leave her own country. And because the child looked the age of their child in the passport it was fated perhaps. It was also fated, wasn't it?, because the woman would never have returned to the country except that she couldn't let her husband go back alone—and only two of them could have carried it off in that country—with its wobbling flat bed trucks and tankers and jitneys and scooters and insane taxis and buses that spewed black smoke and its skinny boys dodging between carts and horses and more carts from which the boys sold boiled eggs inside of which a tiny bird already with pinpricks of feathers was boiled alive as a delicacy—a delicacy!—to be bitten into when the egg was cracked.

What else should they have done? If they allowed the little girl to leave the room, whoever brought her by mistake would take her away to be used again. The authorities were in league with those who brought children to foreigners' rooms. The man and the woman were efficient people and their hearts were broken and they were numb and they had nothing to lose. How else could they have pulled it off?

But then there were the electric sensations that still fuzzed in the woman's fingertips. They had stolen the child who had been sold and otherwise would be sold and sold until she was dead of disease and even the man and the woman were afraid to take her to the doctor now—where to go?—what was to be done? Except that the man had a friend who worked in a clinic and they could possibly approach him, and the woman was thinking that there is a place inside any mother who knows how to help a child, yes, a child is a child is a child, yes.

The woman turned on the light.

The child was standing in the bedroom again. Her nightgown was on backwards. The neckline dipped low on her chest where her breastbone jutted. The woman got out of bed. Getting up like this night after night—oh, suddenly it reminded her of when Allison was a baby waking up all through the night, night after night.

"Come on," the woman said to the girl. "You'll need to turn this around. That's the back. You have to keep warm or you'll get a cold. It's cold here. But that's okay because we make the house warm. Everything is okay here."

The child looked at her with that look—of waiting and calculation.

The woman was so tired.

"Would you like to see—?" she began. "There's a room that maybe you would be happy to sleep in—for tonight maybe. It was a special room and there are stuffed animals in it."

She led the child out of the bedroom without waking her husband.

As she walked upstairs with the child she asked herself: what is my own life worth? A child was saved from disease and death—and enslavement. Who knew what had been done to her?

The woman fumbled for the light switch.

Allison's room in the bright light was full of the lovely accoutrements of a lucky child. The bed with its pink canopy floated at the heart of the room. Stuffed animals were heaped in a jumble on the comforter. The woman felt breathless with pain.

The child ran toward the canopy bed.

When she turned back her face was alive. But she did not point at the pandas or the monkeys or the tigers. She pointed at the shelf of dolls at the head of the bed, as if at last out of her terrible loneliness she recognized what she missed.

"They are beautiful, ma'am," said the child. "They are beautiful girls."

The Swan Princess

When she tried the dress on at the store it looked nice, tight at the waist, not too fussy—and a harbinger of early spring. Now she couldn't help but think of mold. Moldy cheese. Chapels of mold. Sarcophagi. Leaky molding things.

And her heels. She had never worn such outrageously high heels in her life. Was she a crazy woman? A stilt-walker? You had to be an acrobat to stay upright. The elevation—she might as well be a Sherpa. Clouds should be floating right outside her head. She was genetically engineered to be a short woman. Why was she trying to fool nature, balancing all her weight on these idiotic heels?

It didn't help that the parish hall, overflowing with people, moved slowly from side to side like a giant bag of water. Ahead of her, bridesmaids in pastel blue gowns floated by like vapor.

There. There. Right there. Anise. In the center of the hall with that skinny old man in the rumpled suit. Happy, lucky man to be there with the bride. Anise. Anise for whom Julia was here because without Anise's pleading she would never have returned. Oh, Anise, I've lost you inside your mammoth vat of a wedding dress.

Someone tapped her shoulder. The best man. "You certainly can't encounter something like this in New York," he said. He held out a cup of punch to Julia.

She laughed, "You're not going to drink it yourself?"

"Oh no. But as I said, you can't find this in New York." When she didn't take the cup he walked away, his face hardening. She hadn't meant to insult him. She just didn't know what to say. That was one of her problems: that delay she experienced when people talked to her.

The man in the groom's party in a too-big tuxedo—he had a dent in his head as if part of his skull had been removed. He sneezed after he nodded at her. That bunch of men under the exit sign—the tall one kept twitching and shrugging his shoulders as if he was wearing a suit made of monkey fur. Julia's brother might have become like any of them—a big guy who made his presence known.

Well. She was safe, she told herself. Even if she had once been filled with soft down and was sucked empty, nothing unexpected could ever happen in this hall. If she felt awkward, even that was expected. When she and Anise were eighth-graders they served in this hall as volunteer waitresses at a wedding, and Julia had accidentally ladled gravy down the back of a man's suit jacket and never confessed. Her shyness had kept her from speaking up even then.

After all these years there was the same beige paint on the walls as when she was a girl. The same tiles that made the dance floor look like a frozen lake crazed with cracks.

Anise's mother—it would be comforting to find her in the crowd. She had held Julia on her lap and rocked her a million years ago after Julia's brother had strapped binder twine across a plywood board and rigged the board to two inner tubes which were, in their turn, hooked with fence wire. It had been an early almost-spring day, and ice like grits still rimmed the roots where the water ate away tree bark. Julia's brother sat cross-legged on his rigged-up raft and let himself drift on the creek. This was according to a witness who used to work at the grain mill and often wandered the creek bank and passed the boy without concern. Many years ago this man also rafted on the creek and knew its pleasures: how you find yourself veering, hitting against a rock and tipping like a tub toy. Or you're snagged in an overhang and have to pole yourself away with whatever loose branch you can reach.

People lined the creek for miles to look for the body. The next spring they lined the creek again, but they didn't come in memory of her brother. Julia had been stunned by the swans—like pillowcases coming alive and floating off a clothesline to settle on the creek. She remembered white wings rising and unfolding where the creek was fed by the stream behind the parish hall. The swans that arrived that spring were shockingly white, but ugly and ungainly when they tottered across the bank. A decade later she would ask about the swans. Her mother said she didn't remember them. Memory's like that, her mother said, it confuses us. Your father has no memory to speak of anymore, she said. Both of Julia's parents were beyond confusion now.

The woman smelled like tic tac mints.

"You haven't changed at all. You don't remember me. It's Katie Gibbs. Mag's youngest sister?"

"Of course," Julia said before it came back: Katie Gibbs, a spy rifling through her purse when she sat behind Julia at basketball games.

The quartet was tuning up, and Julia couldn't hear what Katie was saying. A hand pressed her shoulder. She turned and saw an older woman in a peach-colored dress with wide shoulder pads. Who was she? Oh—it was Anise's mother. Julia gasped in recognition and thought, What has she done to herself? The vividness Julia remembered had drained from her face.

"I've heard from nearly everyone we used to know," Anise's mother said. The warmth in her voice! "We were so relieved that you could make it."

Julia said something about how glad she was to be there.

Anise's mother cocked her head and said, "I hope you're hungry. All Anise has talked about for weeks is chicken. How we have to have enough chicken and how tough it's going to be to get good chicken. She makes everything difficult. You'd think she'd carried all the hens on her back across a mountain pass. Ask her to tell you about her stones."

"Her stones?"

"She thinks she's a sculptor now. She's got it into her head that she can take something ordinary and just keep it ordinary and people will want it. She makes stones. Ask her."

After her second glass of wine, Julia's knees weakened. She knew that if she stood much longer her legs would go out from under her. Or else she might start laughing at nothing, even at that poor guy walking the outer rim of the hall as if she didn't know he was following her with his eyes.

And then—another sip of wine clearing her head instead of turning it peculiar—she told herself to buck up. Stop it. No one cares. You're nervous and acting paranoid.

It seemed to work—that blast of clear-headedness.

She was glad when she found an empty table. She made herself sit and was soon joined by a young couple. The wife worked at the Bridal Gallery. It turned out that the couple had moved into a new development. Their curlicue of a street was largely empty. Another family chose to design a home with bizarre specificity, down to the cat door, and was suing the developer for failure to comply with their plans. After the couple began to ignore her, Julia found herself staring at a man at one of the round tables. He was seated beside an older woman leaning in toward him. With a start, it came to Julia that she knew him. They had dated once or twice as teenagers. Seated with him was his own mother, who stared at the side of his face with such feeling that Julia endured vertigo. He had to know it was coming, that ball of scorching love. His mother had waited until he was looking away to send it.

"There's something about a candlelight reception," the woman at Julia's table said, out of what struck Julia as an attempt to be polite to her. "It's romantic." The woman turned to her husband. "Where's your sense of romance?"

"You're right," he answered. "Everyone's starting to look surprisingly good." He winked at Julia, and she felt herself blush.

Across the hall Katie Gibbs, her black dress barely covering her thighs, was talking to three men, one of whom was looking over Katie's head at Julia. What could Katie be reporting? Didn't anyone think she'd ever return? She had every right to return. Anise was her friend. Even though Anise was nowhere to be seen. After all, at her own wedding Anise had better things to do than to hover over a friend. Not that Julia needed to be hovered over. And Anise wasn't a hoverer anyway. Anise accepted things. She made everything normal, because she was normal. A relief the way she was so normal. As if you could become normal just by standing next to her. But it was odd, what she was doing with stones.

Julia was thinking about going for a walk on the grounds of the hall when a stream of whiteness rushed toward her. It was Anise, who laughed and grabbed Julia's arm and cried, "Isn't this fun? I should have gotten married a long time ago! You too, Julia!"

But that's not what Julia heard her friend say. Instead, she heard: "Everyone knew. Isn't it funny? A long time ago. Poor you, Julia!"

Julia's throat closed as Anise kept on. "Do you remember that time we jumped into that swimming pool?" When Julia wasn't able to respond, Anise said, "Why did we do that? Oh, I remember. We were possessed." They had jumped into an unattended hotel pool on a school outing to the state capitol. Anise lied and told the teachers they fell in.

"We just wanted attention," Anise said. "We didn't get any." She patted the stomach of her wedding gown. "I feel like an onion in this." To Anise she didn't look like an onion at all, but as if she had been swallowed by a giant white predator that left only her head and wrists visible until she was almost entirely digested.

Julia said, "Your mother told me you made—stones."

"She told you? Oh. I can imagine what she told you."

"She didn't tell me much, really."

"Stones. It can't sound interesting."

"I'm very interested."

"It's not so much about what they look like. It's how they feel when you touch them. I like the way the clay responds. I can go out in the morning and they're wet. Or in the summer in the afternoon they're warm, baked. Plus, they don't do anything. But sit there and take the heat. I admire that. At any rate, I find that kind of wonderful."

"Could I buy one?"

"I'll give you one. They're great to hold. You know what

my mother says about my stones? She says, 'I'll give you this. They look authentic. But honey, they're just fake stones.'"

The sounds from the wedding reception faded behind Julia. The shadows of pines mingled. Birches from fifteen years ago leaned in upon one another. The earth was brittle with a lingering frost crust. Julia would have to be careful to avoid the thawed spots where her heels could sink.

She stepped into a patch of darkness, regretting that she hadn't bothered to return to the cloak room for her coat. The wind against her face, the smell of the pines, the gravel under her heels—all remained achingly familiar. When she was a teenager Julia ran along this path to escape from a boy who had been a friend of her brother. It had been a summer night following an afternoon of thundershowers.

In earlier years, she and Anise used to catch minnows in the stream and watch them swirl in jars. They fished for bullheads and brought them up the road in a bucket, dumping their catch in a horse tank brimming with rainwater. One by one, after days, despite a diet of oatmeal, the fish floated to the top of the tank. Even long after she was forbidden to, Julia came to the stream with Anise. They made their way to the bridge where they might be rewarded with the sight of a muskrat. After crossing the bridge they had a choice: to stay on the road that curved into town or to take the road straight, where the tar ran out. Often they chose the gravel road with its two abandoned houses and a cemetery. In spring the ditches sent up May apples and bloodroot, later quenched in milkweed. In late summer the air grew thick with the bitter smell of new grapes and elderberries. All year long the oaks and the maples were clotted with wild vines.

She was coming close to the stream. A flood must have raided the banks. Trees looked ready to topple, bald roots glowing. A white patch of old snow gripped the end of the path. Beneath each fresh welling-up from the stream, deeper sounds churned.

A shudder went through the gravel at her feet. Pebbles sprayed. The bank sloped under her feet and Julia slid. By the time she caught herself she was kneeling, and the air pulsed with a scorched odor, like plastic burning on a stove.

A wall of whiteness rustled forward. She could hear breathing and then, amazingly, a swan's neck curved and swung close to her forehead. The feathers smelled like old sweat caught in a pillow. She sensed that the swan's feathers would prickle like nettles if they brushed against her.

"What are you going to do?" a voice asked. "Come on, Julia. Everybody knows you're a liar."

The swan's wings lifted and lowered until the air fanned like smoke.

Julia looked through her fingers. The swan's eyes shone yellow with black slots at the centers. The hissing grew into a rasp.

"Don't pretend I'm not here," the swan said. "Bow to the swan king!"

When Julia wouldn't move or answer, the bird wheezed, "There's something under my wing. Help me. Help me. You can."

The swan dipped its beak under its wing. With difficulty, the beak tugged and then, at last, wrenched free.

"Help me," the swan pleaded. Its head began to hang like a blow-up toy leaking air.

Julia made herself reach out. She felt under the feathers, chilled as packed snow. Her fingers cramped. When she pulled her hands away, her fingers were covered with slivers of watery ice, gray feathers, and flecks of blood.

"Look," the swan said, its breath skimming her ear. "Look. You're bleeding."

It was then that Julia flailed her arms and beat at the swan, beat and kicked until the body peeled away and the finest cold white particles fled through the air.

Gray feathery down slid over her fingertips. She brushed her hands over pebbles, but the feathers were sticky, and then, with panic, she stood and stumbled away, half-crouched. She did not look behind herself as she scuttled back in the direction of lights and music.

Julia's heart roared, as if whatever had happened—a blood clot bursting and overwhelming her with a million ragged constellations, a seizure that swung up and through her brain, the nervous breakdown that she had been courting for years—whatever it was could not obliterate her after all.

Over the parking lot hung new snow, like powder blown off a snow bank, suspended in the beams of the lights above the parking lot. The parish hall was illuminated a frosted blue.

At the entrance to the cloak room she stood before the mirror for a long time. The front of her dress looked black where it was wet.

When she turned around, her heart slowed at the sight of lilies floating like white gel lights on the tables. The wedding cake was plundered level to level like a ruined castle—but what a lovely castle. A bridesmaid leaned against a pillar and held hands with a little boy wearing an ivory-colored suit. At the wedding party's table, where candles flickered, the groom in his white tuxedo stared into the center of the hall.

And there on the shining dance floor Anise's father was spinning with his daughter, his hands lost in her dress. The two didn't look separate at all, but like one creature half-sunk in froth. Anise must be tired, must be dancing to please her father. For who can say no to a father? Who can stop a father? Not Julia's poor brother.

It was then that Julia began to make her way to Anise. She didn't know what she was about to do—except that she wanted to strip the arms of Anise's father from Anise. And then, when she was about to reach the pair, Julia skidded toward her friend and her friend's father—both of whom saw her sliding in time to catch her.

They were laughing as she stumbled into their arms, laughing because she looked hilarious: Julia, self-effacing and kind, so clumsy, skidding over in her funny high heels, Julia who had no one. They felt more than a little guilty about Julia, not quite knowing if they could spare the life energy for her—Julia, who must have spilled a drink or two on her dress and who seemed as baffling as ever. But neither Anise nor her father knew why on this happy day they should have felt the startling change, why tears came to their eyes even as they were laughing—Anise holding her friend and her father putting his arms around both young women and swaying to the quartet's version of some song the father didn't recognize, the father who vowed, vowed twice more, that he'd do something for Julia, his daughter's goofy little friend from all those years ago. Standing like this, with his arms around both girls, he vowed that right off he ought to give a donation to the church to fix the damn floor beneath them, treacherous as ice. No wonder Julia slid.

He called his wife over—waved to her and she came, half-skidding herself, to take Julia away. Because somehow his wife knew, always, what to do. Never missed a beat. Saw the big picture. Saw something—although sometimes what she saw— well, it was too late by the time she saw, but at least she saw. He had Julia's hand in his own now, her hot hand, slippery. His wife would help bring this girl down from a wine high, would get her back to normal if anyone could.

Julia, beginning to recover, felt her own breathing slow again as if she could read Anise's father's thoughts. It was clear to her—how could she have thought otherwise, even for a moment—that he was a decent man, and because he was a decent man, he could not imagine his way into the past.

And so Julia knew she was alone. It was left to her to be the one who must try hard to hold to goodness, to Anise's goodness, to Anise's mother's goodness, and to Anise's father's goodness, to hold to them, to imagine in their direction, toward them, toward their innocence, to hold close to those who never had been, and never would be, visited by the swan king.

La Belle Dame Sans Professeur

Many years ago I asked one of my professors at a restaurant—I'd slept with him—if he could buy me something to eat. I was passing through the restaurant to see if I knew anyone there who could help me. For about two-and-a-half days I hadn't eaten anything but popcorn. There were three other professors with my professor, which made things worse, and in my memory the restaurant was loud and dimly lit and my professor was hunched over a plate. As soon as I asked him, my professor said No.

He repeated himself.

Then he said Scat. The way you talk to a cat.

Don't you hate humility? he used to say in class, and I tried to understand what he meant by that. I took notes that looked like this:

> Humility = Boring.
> Very boring.
> Infinitely boring.
> Low energy masquerading as virtue.
> False modesty = everything mediocre people hope
> to be accused of.

Adultery isn't any fun, my professor told me in private, unless it's like a very involved practical joke. He said that at a certain point the wife in our example suspects something, and then the game becomes more rudimentary. Nevertheless, the wife must count to four million before she admits what she knows. Until then she walks around blindfolded and thinks the furniture keeps moving.

He taught literature. Of course.

Under his influence I began to admire Keats, even though he had reservations about Keats. We were here, he said, to conduct, he said, an interrogation. Keats's poems are about breathing, my professor said. Keats was coughing blood while he wrote those lines. He was more aware of breath than any of you will ever be, my professor said. Keats could have been a far more remarkable presence, my professor said, but his early death inhibited his fullest and most dynamic realizations as well as his interrogation of the cultural position he occupied. My professor didn't entirely like Yeats either. Keats. Yeats. They merge, he told us, into Yeast.

Remember the Vikings? my professor asked me, using a peculiar sing-song voice. It was after my fifth class session with him, after Keats had been grilled for the most extensive period. (*Season of mists and mellow fruitfulness.* Pretty—even gorgeous—but a dead end. Part of the problem with the Romantic sensibility, my professor said.) Chalk streaked the front of my professor's jeans. (I work in the chalk mines, he liked to say. I'm in danger of chalk lung, he liked to say.) That day after he asked me about the Vikings he said, What did the Vikings have that you don't have? Confidence!

A week later I was on assignment for the entertainment section of the college newspaper and walked in on Joe Cocker in the Plymouth Stadium dressing room. One of the band members was wearing tight blue briefs. It was embarrassing, but after the band members stopped shouting they nodded at me in a good-natured, almost courtly way. And then Joe Cocker came out from somewhere and shook my hand. I took out my pad and pen and asked him questions (who was your greatest influence? what are your future plans?) and was amazed at how much he looked like my professor—as if he never slept through the night once in his entire life. His eyes were red as if from a permanent case of conjunctivitis.

I told my professor about his resemblance to Joe Cocker and he said, You can't be right. You will never meet anyone like me.

You ought to develop an imagination, he said. Start small. At least lie a little. Lying is a start. Just don't lie to me. Remember this: Great liars in history, they're countless. Tacticians, strategists, managers of any land beyond the size of an acre. Liars, all of them.

In class he turned out the lights and narrated a slide show. Aldous Huxley. Virginia Woolf. D. H. Lawrence. Hilda Doolittle. Virginia Woolf again, looking like a beautiful ferret and wearing around her neck what appeared to be an actual ferret. At one point I wasn't watching the slides but resting my head on my desk. Suddenly the class gasped like one mammoth lung sucking in air. I lifted my head. On the screen was a slide of my professor, staring at the camera, wearing absolutely nothing, in front of a cottage said to have been inhabited by Katherine Mansfield.

He gave me a photograph not long after that. The whole time I held the photograph I could feel his eyes sliding over the side of my face.

The photograph was taken by someone looking down at a woman—leaning over a railing, most likely. A blue and gold blanket appears melted underneath the woman. But the woman in the photograph isn't relaxing on the blanket. She seems stunned, her knees drawn up to her chest, her hands at her ankles pulling herself inward. She is trying to take up as little space as possible in the lens. It had to be his wife.

Keep it, he said. It's yours, he said. Photography is my avocation.

I knew even then that as soon as I got back to my room I would tear the photograph of his wife into bits, as if that would absolve me of the crime of seeing her like that. But when I held the photograph with my professor staring at me I didn't tell him about what I planned to do. Instead I said, This is powerful.

One night before he had to drive home to grade papers my professor said, Tell me a little about yourself. Go ahead. I'm listening. Help me avoid fulfilling my obligations.

I told him about Texas, land of the armadillo, my home state. The armadillo is the dirt bag of the natural world, I said.

I told him I was raised by people who collected people. In the end my adopted parents wound up with twenty-four kids and almost got on the cover of *Ladies Home Journal*. Throughout my entire childhood I was only allowed to wear yellow socks—to make sorting laundry possible. We had three deep freezers in the basement. The woman pretending to be our mother hung a pair of her own pantyhose on the outdoor faucet. Stuffed with bars of Ivory soap for us to wash with. She wouldn't drain the water from a pot of noodles—she was so afraid of losing nutrients. If any of my family saw me now they would call me *disgraced.*

Is that so? he said. They must be the salt of the earth. They'd be pretty shocked, huh? Good. Shock is good.

I didn't tell him that I actually just had one sibling—a brother, and both my parents were alive and well in Havre de Grace. All that stuff about being adopted—it started as a joke meant to make my life sound interesting. It would take me a while to understand that I could have told him I was raised by polar bears or ocelots or Capuchin monks and he wouldn't have found my life interesting.

By the fountain, the day after he told me at the restaurant to scat, I saw my professor. We were outside the library and the fountain was turned off. It looked like a giant cement dog dish. My professor trotted up, sending dry leaves scattering off the path, his coat flapping. There was a nip in the air. It was past time for mellow fruitfulness. The hills behind my professor's head looked scalped.

When my professor opened his mouth, a little spout of a cloud puffed out. Are you still hungry? he asked. The space under his nose lengthened, and I couldn't figure it out. Then I understood: he was trying to make his face leer. It was an almost convincing leer—a self-conscious leer. As if it had all been a joke, as if I was playing a trick on him when I passed through the restaurant and stopped at his table, as if my hunger had been metaphorical.

When I didn't say anything, he said, You're a cute kid, but we've got to stop this.

I know, I said. La Belle Dame Sans Professeur, I said, groaning at my own joke. I couldn't stop myself. I said, My hair is long, my foot is light, my eyes are wild. And then I said, I guess you're not going to find me roots of relish sweet or honey wild or manna dew.

He looked at me as if he didn't recognize I was ruining Keats.

I tried again with more Keats. No birds sing, I said.

My professor looked away. I was sure he didn't recognize Keats's words. As if he didn't read Keats *for* the words. Then my professor said, Take somebody else's seminar next semester. It doesn't look right. Your being in any of my classes. Not good.

I asked him why he cared about how things looked.

He laughed and said, Guess what? I quit smoking. He clapped his hands together.

Again? I said. I could see my breath hanging between us.

Cigarettes and speed—who needs both? he said. I pulled my head back so he couldn't tap my forehead. See you later, my professor said, his coat flapping behind him when he took off.

Before I tried and failed to transfer I sometimes saw him in the distance, walking across the snowy quad.

I changed my major to demography. The study of populations, rather than individuals. After I withdrew from my professor's class, I still took pains to sit in the auditorium so that he was in my line of sight at lectures by visiting scholars. He never went to the readings by poets or fiction writers, only the scholars. Often he was with a graduate student who looked enormously proud of herself, although sometimes he was with his wife. It should have been obvious, but it took me a while to put it together that the woman in the photograph wasn't his wife.

Even as late as last year when I saw his obituary in the alumni news bulletin I still didn't know how to think clearly about the man who had been my professor. I knew, of course, what I was supposed to think. But after so many years I still felt the same enormous sadness for him that I began to feel by the time I left college. Have mercy on him, I kept repeating. As if he was the one who had missed the opportunities, as if I had to be the fortunate one.

Less than a week after I saw the obituary I dreamed that I was leading a tiny man out of a room where he had been held captive for a very long time. The man was blinking and gasping. His hand in mine was moist and trusting.

As soon as I woke up I thought the man must be my old professor. But then, seconds later, I knew better. It was Keats.

The Floating Woman

If I had deliberately caused you pain I would never have forgiven myself. But I would have understood. Do whatever you want to me; it doesn't matter now—was that what you wanted to tell everyone? Your body that couldn't defend itself.

You always said you didn't understand what made me happy. I've come to think that what made me happy was the sensation of expansiveness. That place I went to years and years ago—it's a housing development now, with a display house like a big dollhouse. The land used to be all woods, owned by a man who kept sheep. As soon as I was there I felt like my soul was stretching out of my body and covering the place. That was so long ago, but I felt that I wasn't just this little kid anymore but this spirit, this soul that was large and sealed itself over the place—like a Tupperware lid. You'll laugh at me, but we had Tupperware to think about as a new thing in our house back then. I loved the sound of water passing over pebbles and falling in a lingering way toward the creek where boys made a dam. Once, I was cutting stalks of tiger lilies on the other shore of the creek and my mother was with me, and I thanked the trees, I thanked the sky, I thanked the stream. I did what I did when I was alone, saying my prayers to everything around me until my mother said, "What's wrong with you—."

Darling, that's a question I never dared to ask you.

Please know, though, that I've felt close to you always, even after you left us. I've felt this way most in moments resembling this one, after I plow into the river and turn over on my back and float, and dog-paddle, and float again. I'm resting in the memory of a life where somehow both of us resisted our shame—shame for being so wrong so often and so overly earnest, even you. We were so besotted with Gladys, always planning for her. And now despite our interferences and fretting she has her happiness in Jeff and their little boy. One of the regrets of my life: that you weren't around for that baby. The trustfulness of small children: you would have wanted to see that again. And the easy forgiveness of that little guy when their silky Labrador knocks him over.

So many sensations speed through me from a distance . . . Forgive me. Forgive me, everyone. I haven't forgiven everyone, though, that's for sure. When my aunt said, "Stop pitying yourself" a week after our baby died . . . Oh, I couldn't trust her anymore. I know she thought she was helping me, but I never trusted her again after that. It was as if she poured acid on my heart. If you can't weep when the most terrible thing happens, when can you? My aunt's dead now and I still feel angry at her. So many times I couldn't feel any forgiveness for anyone. Until we had Gladys. Once Gladys and I were having one of our front-lawn picnics and she rested her head against my knee and turned and looked up at me—with that little round dimpled baby face of hers—and I thought—Thank you, God, for her. Thank you for everyone I love.

And there was the time when I learned that my body was my own again, and Dr. Chulamu smiled, and I walked out of his office as if I were on strings and drove to the track at the high school—it was summer, and I was wearing my regular work shoes but it didn't matter—I just kept running and telling myself I am not dying and I am made of air and I didn't stop until my knees buckled and I went down and said Thank you, thank you, life, thank you, I'll live better, and when I got home and walked through the front door you said, "No one and nothing can stop you."

And then the time that our daughter was about to get married and you weren't alive to influence her—the boy was on his way to becoming a monster—and already he wanted to stop her from seeing her friends, and the night before the wedding I couldn't sleep and suddenly she burst into my bedroom and said, "This cannot continue," and she and I drove out of town to avoid the more violent people from his family—and for a month Gladys ("Why did you give her such a little old woman's name?" her groom-not-to-be complained to my face), Gladys stayed with your sister in Washington and I thought, You would be proud of us, you would be proud . . .

Last night I watched *Pal Joey*. I misremembered everything. I thought it ended badly but it didn't.

Do you remember Bruce, who named his baby Ragnar after Ernest Borgnine in *The Vikings*? Ragnar throws himself into the wolf pit. But Valhalla waits. Because he dies with his sword. Initially, they thought he'd drowned in the fjord. It's kind of a toss-up—drown in the fjord or jump into a pit of wolves. Oh, honey.

And do you remember the Christmas display? Three flaking Wise Men. One rubber baby. A camel. Three sheep. A goat. That outsized Frosty the Snowman. And those lights you put up that ran around the house like a frenetic rash? Everything's out in the garage at this time of year and I'm afraid to tell you at every time of year—like a sad little migrant camp. And the dentist who used to live next door and complained about our Christmas lights and the music that came out of Frosty and the dentist used his leaf blower so much that you called him Horatio Fucking Leafblower? Do you remember?

Do you remember when Gladys didn't get to be the jewel in the parish priest's feast day crown? I forgot to mend her red jumper, which would have been perfect for the play, the perfect red for the ruby in the parish priest's crown. Did you know—I don't know if you remember—do you know that she wore that red jumper for the audition, with worn spots in the corduroy and the strap broken and the chief nun looked at her in that perfect red—the color of open heart surgery—and she turned to the little Vatar girl who happened to be wearing a dark but citrusy orange with tiny polka dots like some kind of thrush disease on a lily, and the nun said that the Vatar girl made a better ruby than Gladys did?

That was around the time when you were flirting with the Australian woman and I was sick at heart, and then you came back inside the house from examining the sinkhole in the yard and whispered to me that you found a condom on Frosty's nose—hideous neighborhood kids—and you had scraped the condom off with a stick? The condom must have looked like a little flag of surrender—for a mouse—and after you washed your hands you took Gladys in your arms and told her that you wouldn't want your daughter parading in red like some South Seas maiden in a hula ceremony before a syphilitic missionary and Gladys, thank God, didn't even know what you meant but she stopped crying. And that night in bed when you brought up the issue of the Frosty condom again I turned over and said, "So, Frosty's in love," and I think that did it for the Australian woman. I mean, would she ever have said that? I could feel the air going right out of your desire for that woman at that very moment. So Frosty's in love.

When one is in a bad situation the mind must pause, the mind must relax, and as you always advised me: Just feel, babe, just concentrate on sensations—let your mind rest and then there's hope. Never panic. Why couldn't you have followed your own advice?

It's funny how I remember things. The tiny delicate-looking man in the bar in Malaysia—when we were always traveling somewhere after the baby died and before Gladys came along. That man approached us with such friendliness and courtesy. He was wandering around in the bar wearing a brown suit. "How good to see fellow countrymen," he said. His accent was British. I laughed and told him we weren't his countrymen. "Ah, so I'm among the formerly colonized," he said. "Excuse me, but how good to meet you!" And there it was: that elaborate courtesy we liked so much—and ebullience too, a lightness in his nature like that of a man used to meeting new people and being welcomed. We were on our second scotch when some couples arrived and took the next table over—they were British like him—and one of them said, "He's playing you for drinks." We looked at our charming new friend. What had we been talking about? His adventures in Kuala Lumpur, I think—and he transformed instantly, cowering, sinking lower at the table. "You here, sponging again," someone at the next table sneered at him. And for the first time I really saw the brown suit that the man at our table was wearing and how it was frayed at the cuffs and dirty. His jacket was too small and heavy and buttoned up despite the humid weather.

But you. You ordered the man at our table another drink and said, loudly, "What a gift you've got, man, for a story. My wife's hair is standing on end!"—which was a joke because I was always washing my hair right before bed and when I woke up in the morning my hair had these funny cowlicks. And then we both were laughing, and we made sure to laugh at every joke our new friend told us because, even if he was sponging from us, he was our guest and one of the things we hated most was to see someone made to feel ashamed.

I know that Wesley is usually up early too and takes the boat out and he'll see me out here, far out, and he's made of curiosity . . . Unforgivable of me . . .

I thought that you would never forgive me for so many of my failings—but then, yes, I learned that you would, because one day after we were married for eleven years I turned to you and said, "You are my happiness," and while you hated sentimentality you held your tongue and I saw your neck blush and the blush soak up over your cheeks and I thought, Oh, that I can make you feel this way—I had no idea—because we had taken some wrong turns, but there you were, the whole opinionated breadth of you.

And later, after you weren't with us anymore, I thought: I will reach you again, dear, on the other shore. I knew you would laugh at me—you didn't believe that we had a life after this life—and you were certain of it. If you could talk to me now and I could hear you I know what you would say: *Think straight, Dorothy. Think. You don't swim well, so why have you done this? You shouldn't have been so absent-minded. You have to take account of your limitations. People will think you killed yourself. Don't give them the pleasure. Gladys will be sickened and crazy and confused. What were you thinking, just getting up in the morning and walking out into the water and flopping over onto your back and floating along despite the sneaky current and telling yourself little stories?*

But you can't struggle now. Try for shore, dog-paddle in that hilarious way you dog-paddle, and then before you get tired lie on your back and keep on floating. Keep calm. Remember what I told you when you were punishing yourself so long ago. You said, "I can't help but feel guilty—all the things I haven't done, all the suffering and sadness I haven't stopped when I could have stopped it."

"Do you think you're God?" I asked.

"No," you said. "I don't think I'm God. I just feel so guilty for all I haven't done to help people."

"God's the one who should feel guilty."

I'll say it to you again: God's the one who should feel guilty. Lie back now. Don't be afraid. Fear never helped us at all.

The indignity for Gladys, but she knows me, our Gladys. She has forgiven us, even for giving her such a name. They call her Glad, that's what her friends call her. And it fits her.

I think of Gladys when she was hardly more than a baby, maybe a three-and-a-half-year-old, and we were splashing about together in the bathtub and I was a young mother with her balanced in the tub on my knees, and I wasn't yet grateful for being young, although I was grateful for Gladys. She kept babbling about something and then she cried out in this suddenly mature voice, "Do you think heaven is this nice?"

Did you teach her to say that? I've had my heaven, you used to say—a joke—after a decent meal. Your one bit of hyperbole. You left the other hyperboles to me.

Even now I want to tell myself that you're waking up Wesley, my possible rescuer. You're interceding, bending over Wesley's face, his wet old mouth, making him wake up and decide it's a good day for fishing. It will be good for Wesley, thinking he's saving me.

It is odd, I suppose, to think that it will be good for you too—a rescue. Given your suffering, given that you thought there was no goodness left. Given that you must have thought you were saving Gladys and me from suffering because of how you suffered and how we would have to endure your suffering. Given that you thought you made the right choice for all of us.

But you must admit that we barely saved ourselves after you were gone. Admit that I have not had my heaven because of you. That there were times when I nearly ended my own life. Admit that you must face it, face me: what you did to yourself, to life—what you did will go on forever. But admit that I have never let you leave—listen to me talk to you at any time at all. And that somehow I will see your face again and I'll want to hear your stories. What was death like for you without me? And, laughing, painless, shameless, wrong about everything and free, you'll tell me.

The Bottled Mermaid

I didn't expect to inherit anything at all from my uncle. Certainly I never would have expected to inherit his house. He had had stepchildren, after all, and although it's true that he and their mother divorced and she remarried and her subsequent husband adopted her children, I still felt strange that my uncle would give me his house. Guilty too. The stepchildren, however, weren't forgotten. They had inherited from my uncle the tavern in the lot across from the house.

No other place lived in my memory like my uncle's home and the nearby properties—the woods and the creeks and—a forty-minute walk away—the ocean. He was my mother's brother, and I loved him, but it was his house I remember best. Even before I returned I could describe every room's wallpaper. And the shelf that was carved to look like its edges were festooned with grapes and grape leaves. And the horsehair chair that always scared me in a delicious way, as if a giant bear had taken up residence in my uncle's living room. And even the room he kept closed, the windows shuttered, because it was a shrine to my mother. He kept many photographs of her there and lumps of turquoise and tiny sculptures and wooden rosaries she had sent him from her travels with my father.

For nearly three years after my parents' death, and starting when I was eight, my uncle took care of me. Then my father's parents sought custody.

I have never been so unhappy as when I left my uncle. My grandparents were well-meaning but joyless and judgmental people. Their attempts to mold me only made me unhappier. In my memory I cried for what might have been months. I missed not only my uncle and his house but the plum trees on his lawn and the fields behind the house and the long walk to the ocean, and I missed my freedom, given that I was generally unsupervised while my uncle was busy with the tavern.

From my uncle I learned many things that were important to me: how to catch and clean a fish and make a campfire in the woods and cook the fish right there; how to find beer bottles on the roadside and turn them in to the tavern and get quarters; how to grow catnip and make catnip tea.

After my grandparents gained custody I wrote to my uncle but received no letters back. I was never sure at the time that my letters weren't confiscated. Then something went wrong. My uncle got into "trouble with the law." Every year I thought about my life with him less and less.

I was my uncle's only living blood relative, and I learned about his death and my inheritance days after my accident. My medical bills from the accident were astonishing. For months I could hardly afford rent. Having the house and a little extra money from the inheritance saved me.

As for my uncle's stepchildren: their names were Conor and Glynnis Alberon. During the last summer that I lived with my uncle they had the run of the property. Although Conor must have been my age and Glynnis two years younger, they called my uncle by his last name: Dewey. Conor and Glynnis were beautiful golden beings. I was always hiding my face in a book to protect myself from them. The girl was a tiny ball of anger and need. The two of them came in and out of focus unpredictably: watching me, the boy pained and careful with his sister, both of them with every gesture and every glance taking possession of my world. By then my uncle was falling in love with their mother. They must have known that my world would soon become theirs.

I discovered a few things about their subsequent lives before I arrived to settle into the house. Glynnis worked at the bakery in the town center and lived with her brother, and Conor had already been bartending at the tavern for nearly a year before my uncle's death. Conor was a widower, although it seemed strange to call such a young person a widower. His wife had drowned the previous winter, which must have led to all sorts of speculation, given the oddity of a drowning in that season. She was an artist of some sort and her name (she had kept her maiden name) was Anita Ellemenz. After I moved into my uncle's house I made sure to introduce myself to both Conor and Glynnis when they were pointed out to me by the lawyer who handled the estate. They were sitting at a table at the bakery where Glynnis worked, and the introduction was pretty perfunctory. I couldn't be sure that they actually remembered me.

What was obvious: they weren't golden anymore. Their hair had darkened the way blond hair will. But their eyes were the same, and Conor, especially, was a remarkably beautiful person. He struck me as the sort of man who ignores common advice. The sort who's allergic to routine. The sort who mutters funny comments under his breath at public lectures. His face was wide, unlike his sister's narrow, bony one. She hardly blinked, which was unnerving. Conor had Glynnis's pale coloring, her almost translucent skin.

After I saw them at the bakery I looked up Conor's wife's obituary on-line. Then, from earlier editions, the news report. The discovery of a body, drowned. A blurry photograph. The estate's lawyer had remarked that Conor's wife had looked a little like me, and he was right.

For the rest of that first morning when I took possession of the house I ambled around the property. The sky appeared to be a cold opal, the only break in the clouds a nearly undetectable pink sheen. I hadn't noticed it before, but almost invisible under a shrub next to the old swimming pool was the birdbath that I had loved as a child. Seahorses held up a scallop shell for birds to drink from. That day the shell was dusted with snow. Somewhere there's a picture of me as an eight-year-old beside that birdbath, with the swimming pool behind me. I'm looking proud, as if I discovered the seahorses and dragged them up from the ocean floor. We hadn't used the pool often back then. My uncle discouraged me from swimming in it.

In the afternoon I walked the beachfront east of the town center. The wind made my eyes water. Never turn your back on the sea—one of my uncle's warnings, after a giant wave pushed me face down many years ago, trapping me as it withdrew. I had been ten at the time, and the wave's violence seemed human to me, willed. I was more careful after that.

Two figures in the distance advanced toward me. As soon as I recognized them I looked away and toward the ocean, blood drumming in my temples. Fog began puckering and denting over the water. I was nearly at the boardwalk by the lower dunes when I allowed myself to turn, making sure my eyes were dead in case Conor or his sister glanced in my direction. It felt stupid to be acting the way I had when I was a child, but I wasn't able to help myself.

That night I couldn't sleep for a long time. I lay awake in that peculiar florescent zone of insomnia.

Then I thought of Ana Su, and cheered myself up. When I lived with my uncle I had made one friend—or one "almost friend": Ana Su. It wasn't that Ana Su and I talked. We watched each other. We watched each other with that sure sense some children have, as if we were deadly enemies and yet invested in one another's lives. Sometimes I'd be walking on the pier and she'd be walking toward me. We walked very slowly until we met and wordlessly passed one another.

And then so many years later, during the week of my accident—out of the blue—she contacted me, and we began an email correspondence. She was living in Oregon but promised to visit me when I got settled at my uncle's house.

The next night I looked out the window of the second-story landing into The Cavern's parking lot and counted seven cars. Once it was midnight and I had pestered myself for hours about my lack of courage, I threw on my coat and scarf. As soon as I entered the tavern my eyeglasses steamed up, dissolving everything in front of me. I endured the crush of bodies behind me as I was pushed into the barroom. Then I leaned against a wall and wiped fog from the lenses with my gloves and put my glasses back on. The bar assumed a shape. A group of men, three of them with beards, were looking up expectantly. It was in the air—that crimping of the atmosphere—when a woman enters a room where too few women are.

The couple behind me—they were the ones who pushed me in—maneuvered past, apologizing.

Tables were clustered in the center of the bar and in two alcoves. A stream of light from a still-illuminated St. Pauli Girl's sign sped across bottles ranged on shelves. Despite feeling watched the whole time, I examined the bottles. Deep inside each quivered a tiny clay face, wincing in a trick of light. In each bottle: a mermaid.

My reflection bent in the third bottle, and I was thankful that the scar that runs across my forehead and the light scars that cross from my left ear almost to the center of my chin weren't visible in that light. For weeks after the accident when I saw myself in a mirror I thought of a paper doll cut apart by a mean child.

In one bottle, a mermaid, her tail glittering with mirror scales, was propped against a tiny ship. Inside another bottle a model of the same ship was tilted under paper waves, a tiny mermaid huddled next to the hull. At first I imagined that the bottles dated from at least three or four decades ago—given the faded little figures inside, orange-red. Then I realized that probably the figures were only crafted to look old. Something about the bottles was powerful, as if they fizzed with bees.

I navigated to an empty table, and before I could extricate myself from my coat, a stranger was walking toward me. "From Conor," he said, setting down a beer. Conor, his back to me, was busy at the cash register.

The beer was dark and thick-tasting. I felt cold and put my coat back on.

By the time I finished my beer I was waved over to their crowded table by the couple who came in behind me. I landed among talkers, and I was relieved that I didn't have to do anything but listen, or pretend to listen. I pulled off my coat again, helped with the sleeve by one of the men. There was an instant's quiet. Embarrassed, I looked down. The copper color of my shirt appeared fleshlike. I crossed my arms.

There was a discussion about the McCaff Bridge, the bootery, the Condoms Galore Store in some town I'd never heard of. Another beer appeared at my elbow. I looked around to see whom to thank. Someone tapped my arm and said, "Don't try to imagine who that's from."

It was then that Glynnis appeared. The skin under her eyes looked darker and more sunken than ever, the rest of her face more translucent. "Have you been defecting to Squalls?" she asked. "I've never seen you here before." Two of the men at the table pushed their chairs back. One swung up a chair from another table for her.

"No," I said. "Squalls must not have what you have. I bet they don't have mermaids." The skin around her eyes crinkled. "Do you know who made them?" I asked. "Did you?"

"Those bottles on the walls?" she said. She took a while before answering, long enough for me to wonder why. "No. No, I don't know who made them. Can I take your photograph?" She unzipped her coat, and there her camera was, hanging around her neck like a giant cowbell. After she finished taking my photograph and then taking pictures of everyone at the table she said, "Come over to the house sometime. I mean it. I'll show you my work. I've photographed everyone in town." She printed her address on a napkin.

I hadn't meant to wait until the bar closed, but I did, and I was glad when Conor offered to walk me across the lot to the house. His face was perfectly molded, his eyebrows paler than his hair under the streetlight. In the night air, the chill tightened everything. Further inland there would be snow.

"What happened?" he said. "Something happened to you."

"You mean my face?"

"What about your face? You're alone for some reason. Divorce?"

"No. Not that."

"I remember you. The kid with the big glasses. You seemed superior—self-contained. Scary."

It was easy to laugh with him. "The picture you're painting is so different from my memory," I said. "I remember the house most—and my uncle. I saw your sister again tonight. I didn't know she was a photographer. She's a mainstay at the bakery, right?"

"Muffins don't fight back. It's a good job for her. She's not exactly commended for her patience. She doesn't have what used to be called a trusting nature. The trouble is that more than half the time she's right. But only a little more than half the time. She's always been like that. Suspicious. She won't even drive. I have to drive her everywhere."

"She doesn't trust herself?"

"She doesn't trust other drivers. It makes her nervous that they'll cross the center line."

I thought of my accident. "Maybe not trusting other drivers—maybe that's smart."

We stopped on the walkway next to the swimming pool. The blue tarp covering the cement looked frosted and billowed in the wind. "I nearly drowned in there," Conor said, laughing. I remembered what I knew about his wife. It felt odd laughing with him about a drowning. "I was never in any real danger," he said. "Your uncle was there—and my mother and Glynnis were there too."

"That would have scared everyone to death. Especially your mother."

"My mother never quite forgave Dewey for letting me in the pool. She was very good at holding a grudge."

The kiss was so sudden and quick that I drew back, stunned. Conor laughed and so did I. Laughing was easy with him.

Since the accident I had been having headaches. The headaches and/or the dizziness could come on at any time. The worst thing wasn't even the headaches or the dizziness. It was the accompanying nausea, and then the depression. I felt very fragile and, at the same time, angry at myself for being fragile.

Nothing was spinning the next morning, which was good, given that so many things in the antique and craft store where I was wandering were made of glass: blue willow plates so faded they look smudged, salt and pepper shakers in the form of roosters, ducks, beagles, pickles, Liberty Bells. I thought that there might be something that Ana Su would like as a gift.

The shop owner was ignoring me in a way that seemed purposeful as I scrutinized beer steins decorated with wolves. There were two shelves of what appeared to be local craft projects: candle holders glued with gingham ribbons and bespattered with glitter, giant jugs decorated with silver thimbles and golden bells. It struck me as pretty wonderful that the imagination is so entertainingly weird, addicted to making beauty or acquiring beauty or what seems like beauty. Beauty being so various.

Behind a row of cocktail decanters, something came into focus. A terrarium?

Then I understood: it was a bottled mermaid, like the ones in the tavern. Under golden clouds a mermaid rode inside a ship with ragged sails. The mermaid's face was tiny, beady-eyed. It was the same face as those on other mermaids in the bottles at The Cavern. The mermaid's arms were raised. In joy? Triumph? In the foreground, white-capped waves glittered in frosting-thick paint next to a tiny lighthouse. It was a clever little lighthouse—primitive, sweetly sloppy, tilting.

The owner sidled up beside me, his white mustache lifting. "It's original art. Locally made. It's a pretty fancy piece, huh?" He sucked in his breath as I examined the glass. In the lower left corner, cracks rayed outward like a spider's web. "There's a discount," he said.

I ran my fingers around the base and peered into the low shoreline of sand and pebbles for a signature. Nothing. I already knew that I would rescue the mermaid from her dusty obscurity, rescue the wonderfully silly lighthouse and the paper ship.

"Where did you find this?"

The shop owner cleared his throat before announcing, "It's called The Underwater Dance." Sensing a sale, he stepped closer. "There was a set of these. But this one—the man who bought the others didn't have room."

I knew he was lying. There was room at the tavern. My uncle didn't buy this mermaid because he must have predicted that the crack eventually would grow, covering the face of the glass.

"You sold the set to The Cavern?"

The man blushed. "You must have heard all about this."

"No. I didn't. Can you tell me the name of the artist?"

"You're not superstitious are you? Tell me you're not superstitious. Sometimes troubled people are especially creative."

"I'm not and I'm buying this—if you'll tell me."

"There's no need for bribes."

Given that I suspected Conor's sister had lied to me at the tavern I took a guess. "A woman named Glynnis Alberon made this."

"No. Alberon wasn't the last name. Her name was Elle-menz. There used to be these bottles for sale in a lot of places. This is probably the last one left anywhere. There's a light inside, by the way."

On Thursday morning as soon as I got up I noticed that the bottled mermaid was missing from the foyer's buffet. I had placed it there, visible from the window, visible from the tavern.

There were suspects. The oil company workers had been in on Wednesday, three of them, with buckets and lights, equipped like miners to do the furnace cleaning. To make it easy for them to come and go, I had left the front entrance unlocked. Nevertheless, only one name kept returning as the culprit: Glynnis, who might rationalize stealing the bottled mermaid, believing that she was the true natural owner because her sister-in-law, Anita Ellemenz, had made it. After all, Glynnis had lied to me in the tavern, saying that she didn't know who made the bottled mermaids. Somehow she still seemed as enraged and needy as when we were both children.

At the tavern she had asked me to visit her. Which is what I did. I must have thought I could retrieve the bottled mermaid—and possibly present it to Conor as a gift, even though if Glynnis had stolen the thing it would already be in the house they shared. It was an odd fantasy I was having. I wanted to give Conor something, and it seemed that the bottled mermaid was rightfully his. Actually I don't entirely know what I was thinking when I headed out.

The house was a small ranch-style place. Hanging from the porch were pots of dead gray ferns that must have frozen weeks ago. I felt a blast of guilt and also a shameful blast of self-satisfaction. The house I had inherited was so much more welcoming.

Glynnis answered the bell.

"Conor didn't mention you'd be coming," she said. "He'll be home soon."

"Actually I came to see you." I didn't want to pretend I was clueless about her lie to me at the tavern. I was hardly inside the house before I said, "I found out who made the bottled mermaids. When we were at the tavern why did you say that you didn't know who made them?"

"I didn't feel like talking about Anita then. Is that hard to understand?"

She didn't sound like someone who mourned her sister-in-law.

We walked through a formal dining room—blond wood, a low chandelier over a table, brocaded chairs—and into a narrow hall. We passed into what looked like a den. What stopped me short: shelves lined with clay figurines rose to the ceiling. Shelf upon shelf of a frozen city, tiny statues clustered, like fertility objects. The figurines were the same tint as the mermaids in the bottles. When I peered closer it became clear that each figure was at least subtly different, each incised to reflect an original soul.

"Are there any statues of men?"

"No. Anita always said she couldn't do men's faces. She felt safer with women's faces. Big mistake there."

"What do you mean?"

"Women are every bit as unsafe as men."

"There aren't any mermaids."

"She thought the mermaids needed to get out of the house, I think. She probably would have made a lot more to sell if she could have—if. Well, she was a mermaid herself—a beautiful swimmer." She gasped and muttered, "What am I saying?" She pulled a figurine from the shelf and held it out to me. "Isn't this one cute? It's my favorite. That's exactly what I looked like as a kid. Anita worked with photographs. Not just actual people. Old photographs too. She collected them from anyone who would hand them over. I don't think these are like voodoo dolls at all—although I used to."

I was sure that I had come upon something telling, that these legions of figurines were made to protect those whom Conor's wife loved. Possibly she made them to protect herself. The opposite of voodoo—not to harm others but to protect them. Good luck totems. An army of Amazons.

A tightening sensation around my forehead began. I needed to leave before the dizziness started. Glynnis protested, "Why do you have to go so soon? Look at this. There's a box of the photographs she used for some of these. Here. It's pretty inspiring." It was on the third shelf, a photograph box. "You'd be surprised. The whole town is here."

I hurriedly glanced through the photographs without, at first, recognizing anyone.

"This is my mother."

"What did you say?" Glynnis asked.

"Just that they're beautiful."

It was a washed-out snapshot. A close-up. My mother's soft eyes, startlingly dark. A smile about to skim over her face. The photograph was probably taken by my uncle. I recognized the porch pillars at the house. My uncle would never have parted with such a photograph. Someone must have stolen it.

I don't think that Glynnis saw that I took the photograph. Although later it became clear that she'd wanted me to see it. That day, she hadn't offered to show me any of her own photographs.

By the time I stepped outside the sky was dark. A dog howled in the distance. Walking toward my car, I felt pushed to hurry by an invisible hand. I was at the base of the driveway when I was caught in headlight beams. Conor pulled alongside in his truck before I could get into my car.

"Hey," he called. "You're here. Come on up."

"I was just up," I said. "To see Glynnis. I have to leave." I wanted to stay, of course—for him—but not while Glynnis was at the house.

Time passed slowly for the next few days. Conor didn't stop by, and I couldn't find enough energy to cross the lot and see him at the tavern. I was a sick woman who knows she is a sick woman, and I couldn't understand why. *There's nothing wrong with me other than headaches—I have no reason to be like this.* The bromides, the pep talks I gave myself, all the bracing level-headed advice, the stoic urge toward self-forgetfulness— none worked. I went into the city and saw my doctor. She gave me another prescription for the headaches, but I got dizzier and decided it was better just to sleep as often as I could. Which I did.

It was a Friday night when I heard something inside the house—a low, scuffing sound, as if an animal had gotten in through an upstairs window. I had been warned at the realtor's office that squirrels once invaded the attic, although a pest control agent inspected the place before I moved in. I climbed to the third floor and stopped inside the smallest bedroom, taking in the air of use: the rumpled coverlet, the bedside table with the lamp drawn to the edge. On the shelf above the bed, on its side, rested a tiny ship with paper sails. I searched the shelves above the bed, opened the drawer on the bedside table, pulled back curtains, ran my hand along the windowsill.

When I opened the closet door I saw the lighthouse and the empty bottle. The bottle's paper clouds were shattered into confetti. And far back against the closet wall the clay mermaid was propped. Her face looked grated.

Glynnis's voice came from behind me. "Everything will dry out."

I couldn't stop myself from shuddering as I turned around.

Glynnis went on, "There were spots where the paint was too thin and so those parts have to dry. And I was making you new clouds. I was going to surprise you."

When I didn't respond she said, "I don't steal. I'm just fixing this for you. It'll be better than ever. Nothing taken. I don't take things. I'm not the one who steals things. This was supposed to be a surprise."

It is a surprise, I was thinking. Everything is a surprise.

At last I was able to ask, "How long have you been in this room?"

"I've always loved this room. Why not fix the bottle here? I didn't mean to scare you. This room is—soothing to me. This is where Conor and I went after he almost drowned. Dewey didn't try to save him. Afterwards my mother brought us up here and left us. She was screaming at Dewey downstairs while we were up here. But here the screaming was muffled. And Conor and I were safe."

I could almost imagine the scene, although Glynnis must have misunderstood what happened. My uncle would never have wanted to harm anyone. "Does Conor believe my uncle wanted him to drown?"

"We've never talked about it. But I saw. People have always tried to hurt Conor. People tried to hurt Conor and blame him for what happened to Anita, but it wasn't his fault. She was always nervous. She let everything scare her."

I pointed to the closet where orange dust powdered the floor. I asked what she had done to the mermaid's face.

"I wanted to change the face. It's my face Anita used. Anita was obsessed with my face. I changed this one to be like your face."

Glynnis pulled back the bed's coverlet. From under a pillow she drew a photograph album. "I've been keeping this here—so no one sees. Yet. It's not done. But if you look at it even at this point you'll see something you should know about—about your uncle."

I didn't want to look at her photographs.

The cover of the album was black, a mock crocodile skin, the fabric greasy under my palms.

Glynnis said, "The photos—you'll see. I photographed everything Dewey did." She nodded at the album. "It's almost full. You can see. You should see it."

I had to will myself to open the album.

Page after page: photographs of stranger's faces, eyes closed. A pale yellow nipple. More women, their naked bodies melted-looking and flat. My uncle's face was there, almost out of the picture—but it was his face. And probably his hand, the white cuff of his shirt.

In the next photograph glass shattered around a woman's body, the pavement glinting, wet-looking. And then I was the woman in the photograph, and above me the world was stunned with light.

The close-up of the face—my own face. Fluid trickled,

dark against my mouth.

And then I realized it was Anita Ellemenz's face. The edge of the photograph: a gleam, like a watermark. Across it sprayed flecks of white.

I was still looking at the photograph when Glynnis's footsteps clattered down the stairs. I could hear the back door close.

Another photograph: Anita Ellemenz, her face underwater. In the corner of the photograph, blurred: a circle. A drain. The reflection of a white gate.

The shock of seeing the photographs—shock overrode my reason. Even so, after a while I could tell that the women in the photographs were not real, the colors and proportions off. Each like a scene from a dream in which everything is out of scale. An arm was superimposed. My uncle's arm. His face wasn't right either. The proportions didn't match the rest of the scene.

The images were Photoshopped.

Even so, I couldn't stop gasping for breath. The photograph of Anita in the water. The reflection. Her image was superimposed on what appeared to be the swimming pool at the house.

I couldn't know what Glynnis had feared more: that I would not stop loving my uncle in memory, or that I would never leave the house that she loved almost as much as I did. I did know that I wasn't the weak person she imagined. But then, for years I hadn't been the person I imagined I was either.

The developer who bought the house and property I inherited paid a good price. But he was not able to find the necessary backing after the house was bulldozed.

I called Ana Su before I left town. We have so much in common that we couldn't stop talking for hours. I told her about selling the house. Even as we talked I felt stabs of sadness but also something like relief.

Now in my imagination the property fills with tall thistles, shaking their armor. Because the land has been neglected, more weeds set in—milkweed and broadleaf plantain. The lot is like an untended grave, a grave of black weeds. Nothing passes through the yard, except for drunks staggering out of the tavern. Where the plum trees once stood the ground looks charred and glitters with broken glass. And where there aren't weeds there are deep tracks from bulldozers.

The story that my grandparents managed to make me overhear years ago at last struck me as true: my uncle had accepted their bribe. He had been on the cusp of taking on a ready-made family. Taking care of me would have been difficult then. Everything must have begun to shatter that last year I lived with him. It wasn't only my shyness that kept me away from those children who were always around the house. It was fear, even though I couldn't have said what I was afraid of. My inheritance might have been a way for my uncle to assuage his guilt, his guilt for giving away, against her wishes, his sister's child.

The house that I loved, the freedom I loved, my uncle: no longer can I see them even in my imagination in the light I knew from childhood. Even so—and for me there is always an "even so," or a "just the same"—when I think of the selling price of the house and how I'm no longer in debt I feel enormously grateful to my uncle. I feel comforted, too, when I imagine the plot of land as if it's a riverbed that has dried up, and yet a place where a breeze scatters pollen freely.

Before I left I boxed everything from the room my uncle had kept as a shrine. I knew Glynnis had not triumphed—even if she had long ago wanted to replace me, that she had always longed to wreck any claim I had on the house and on my uncle. What she guessed about my feelings for Conor had something to do with it all too.

Ana Su keeps telling me that I did the right thing—that it wasn't revenge so much as good sense. Although I would be entitled to revenge, she says. She confessed over the phone that the summer after I left she got inside my uncle's house and looked around for me as if I had to be hiding there somehow, as if it was a lie that I had ever left.

She promised that next summer we'll take a trip together. We haven't figured out where we're going. She's bringing both her daughters.

The Last Satyr

The satyr apologized to whatever powers cast him into the human world as the last of his kind. He apologized for despoiling, yanking, mewling. For adopting the language and mannerisms of every woman he touristed, for "shedding on the camp bed," for "sundry pharmaceutical trips." For his preference for the wives of easily dissatisfied men.

It was on the curdling skin of the swimming pool that he caught sight of the future—his gruesome hairy face out of which his eyes winced. He told himself he did not want to know why at some future moment he was wincing. The water flashed and sparkled and the future disappeared, filling instantly with the reflection of a diving board.

In the last half hour no one had so much as wetted a fingertip in the swimming pool. The people who were here earlier had set their drinks on glass tabletops. They let the early evening spill around them and stared into the pool where aspen leaves drifted onto the surface and spun. They never knew he crouched in the shrubbery. Eventually, they crumpled their cocktail napkins and pushed back their metal chairs and left.

Fortunately, the remains of their drinks had not been collected. The satyr tossed down two fruit slushes, more ice than rum, and a daiquiri that had been held between the forefinger and thumb of an executive assistant with a fever. Before he lurched onto a reclining chair, he could feel the contours of the thin lips of the woman who sipped from the rim of a scotch.

Shadows and light drifted from a window in a building past the walkway. A woman stood on the other side of the window, inside the building. She had to be looking through reflections—the reflection of the room behind her cast in the window, the further reflection of the glass tables surrounding the satyr at poolside.

Then she did something astonishing that startled the satyr into pure panicked wakefulness. She waved. The window banded with new shadows, and she stepped back.

The satyr clambered off his chair, hustling to the shrubs near the side of the pool farthest from the building. His thighs soon ached from crouching. When he was satisfied that the woman would not appear, he edged out and stumbled to a reclining chair.

The expulsion of breath beside him nearly caused him to reel out of his chair.

"Hey, boy," a woman's voice said. "I can hardly watch them anymore. Can you?"

Her expectancy corkscrewed into him. There it was—that human pressure, as if they couldn't leave anything alone, nor could they see what he actually was. "The pace people keep. They dance like weevils." She raised her chin in the direction of the window. "Look at them. People are never more revealing than when they dance. Not that I can dance anymore, but at least I acknowledge my limitations."

The satyr nodded. He wondered if in the darkness he could pass for an unusually hairy, hunch-backed man.

The woman stared at him so intensely that he feared she might become alarmed and scream. He could see it: men would barrel out of the building. Already he could feel their fists digging out clumps of his flesh. If they knocked his head against the table his jaw would snap. Blood would well from the corners of his eyes.

Every hair on his ancient body was as sensitive as a cat's whisker. The old injury to his knee woke up, and the satyr groaned.

"My feelings exactly," the woman said. "I was sick to my stomach and in bed all day. For a while I felt like running away from my own stomach. Then I was fine at 8:30 tonight. Just like that. This is my retirement gift—this trip. They gave me a party last month. You start to realize that your funeral will be like your retirement party: the same people thinking they've got something on you just by surviving."

The sound of a piano being played floated in from the restaurant. "You can tell a lot about people by the way they treat you when you can no longer hurt them," she said. "I guess it was all my fault. I worked in Personnel. In the end there was hardly anyone I hadn't hired."

She patted her thigh and stared at the satyr as if she expected him to scoot over close to her. "Chester. At my retirement party he recited Yeats. 'That is no country for old men,' he said. He meant, This is no company for old women. This is not your company, Louise. Then he went on about 'those dying generations.' And then 'an aged man is but a paltry thing.' Die, I thought, you can die now, Chester, you bastard. We're waiting. And then it came: 'a dying animal'—and he meant me."

Somewhere, a door opened and closed.

"You never know what uses you'll be put to," the woman was saying. "Even Yeats. What a marvel Yeats was. *But I was young and foolish, and now am full of tears. For the world's more full of weeping than you can understand.* And oh yes: *There is not a fool can call me friend, and I may dine at journey's end with Landor and with Donne.* You hear lines like that and it's easy to remember what a randy bugger he was."

The wind came up and died instantly. The smell of chlorine crept into the satyr's nose. The woman whispered to herself. Gradually her voice grew audible. "I let him have his moment of fun. He thinks he's the only one alive who's ever read a book. I could have recited my Frost imitation and directed it at him: Whose accounts these are I think I know. He keeps a cheap whore in a bungalow. Even a halfwit, say, an accountant, must think it queer—the way he keeps so much in arrears. Two accounts diverge and I—I've made copies of every one of his files—and that will make all the difference."

A breeze passed across the wet stubble around the satyr's lips, and he let himself think about women he had known. The more fragile the woman, the more her dreams led her life for her, sprouting city parks and luxury resorts and residential complexes. Such women were like nymphs. Except that nymphs are in disguise permanently, drawing themselves into tree bark, into lavender, into clover. If you were lucky, a nymph materialized. Even then, even as marbled tissue, in another second she was as hollow as a reed. At the most licentious gatherings—rose petals and oils, fat dribbled into the open cavities of corpses, at those ceremonies in which human men degraded bodies—nymphs stood apart. Suddenly he saw the face of the woman before him as if it were swept underwater, a surprised face disappearing, at the exact moment she was caught. Yes, he could have known her. That might be what her problem was.

Being here, the woman was saying, made her think of that cruise with Les, before being tugged back into port. Who could tell when either of them wasn't drunk? They were out on "the high seas," as Les said, where everything dipped and swelled. Back home in the condominium, a new widow only a week later, she felt it again: a rocking in her body, as if the sea were lodged permanently in her blood.

She was talking so quietly that he tilted his head to hear her. Oh no, she was saying, she never guessed her life without Les would be like drowning perpetually. And no one *saw* her, no one noticed. If they could see her suffering what would they do? Nothing. Everyone suffered. So what? She was lucky. Very lucky. Everyone just wanted her to retire. The barbarians gave her a party. And what holds her heart together? Les—they don't make them like that anymore. "The end of a line," she said.

The satyr didn't think the woman would ever stop talking when abruptly she patted the top of his head before he could pull away. Standing, she lost her balance and grasped at the wadded fur of his shoulder blades with her feeble, half-hollow hand. "Even so," she said. "Even so. I hate my own self-pity. You're almost a comfort to me, you almost are." She sighed. "Do you belong to anyone?" She felt around his neck. He twisted away from her. "Be a good boy and let me check if you have a collar. All right. Have it your way."

On the walkway past the pool the woman turned and cried out, "You're a good boy. Yes, you are."

When she was out of sight, the satyr rested his head on the glass tabletop.

It was she who touched his shoulder. He hadn't meant for it to happen. How could he be blamed? His gift to a dying woman was a restless heart.

Lee Upton

He walked to the edge of the pool, kicking away a pair of flip-flops. A white towel was coiled on the cement. Someone had swum in the pool today for almost forty minutes. In his mind he saw her—a scar on her thigh. Her cell phone rang on one of the glass tables on the other side of the pool. She dropped her towel on her way to answer it.

He looked into the water and closed his eyes, then opened them again. The image he had seen in the pool before the old woman came out was his own reflection—now. It was himself, his shadow reflected by torchlights at the pool's edge. Rippling across the length of the pool, like a dolphin coming toward him, was the future.

The satyr saw everything that would happen, saw himself scratching at the old woman's door until she let him in. Saw himself climb up onto the bed to match his breathing to hers. As if he were hovering close to the ceiling of the hotel room, he saw the woman's mouth fall open. Her brown-veined arm was flung across the animal lying beside her on the bed. In the morning the woman from housekeeping would find the woman and her dog. The unmistakable stillness.

It was inscribed in fate, in an ancient light, by the gods no one anymore could see, although their kind, unlike his own, would never grow extinct, those gods who would allow him what they never needed to worry about for themselves.

Among them were gods of love. And they would not let him die alone.

Bashful

Shana was in her bathtub when her arm brushed across her right breast and she felt the lump. A nearly perfect circle. She didn't tell Rachel what happened. She didn't tell how the air grew cold and—it was too theatrical to be believed—a dark wing passed over her. Through the doctors' visits and even later, Shana was submerged under the memory of that wing, cold and wrinkling, like a bat wing.

The results came back negative. She was relieved that the signal was the wrong signal, but there was a residual sensation she couldn't make go away. She tried to explain it to herself as an inevitable aftermath. She knew she should be grateful, but instead she often felt the bat wing cross her forehead again, and then she was lost and crying.

Eventually Shana told her friend Rachel about the false alarm, but not about the ridiculous wing. The two women worked together at the city's cultural center. Rachel was the oldest in a family of five, which gave her a sixth sense for weakness. It was Rachel who proposed that she and Shana take a vacation together. Shana had no one to turn to, after all. Shana had never even had a serious boyfriend after her divorce. Besides, Rachel didn't like to vacation alone. She was settling down after her own divorce, and her siblings weren't

Lee Upton

in crises at the moment. There seemed nothing more compelling to Rachel than getting Shana back to the land of the living by going down to Orlando.

And that was how Shana found herself dragging about in the lower waters of a man-made lake while Rachel was in one of the resort's satellite buildings getting her second massage of the day.

The lake was so low that yards ahead of Shana the water didn't rise above the shoulders of a man there. Yesterday a group of women Shana and Rachel met over brunch had walked halfway across the lake without getting their hair wet.

The sun lit the man's back and Shana thought she was seeing Jack. But Jack was a thicker man, with a thick neck. A thick neck to hold up his large head. The unmistakable intelligence of his forehead. No. The man in the lake was slightly built. He could never be Jack.

Shana wasn't wearing her contacts, that was part of the problem. She had frightened herself for no reason. And disappointed herself, for why should her former husband terrify her anymore? She had hoped that after undergoing the false alarm she would learn to be stronger and wouldn't repeat the mistakes of the past—all that yearning gone awry, all that passivity in the face of a man who at first wanted her so much. She should be grateful, not frightened. She should grasp her life and stride briskly into the future.

It sounded like a wave was coming in from an outboard motor. The man Shana mistook for Jack disappeared under the water. Such a relief that he wasn't Jack—Jack, who had been so endlessly disappointed in her. Before she could defend herself, the vision of Jack's face rose, and in her imagination he looked more disappointed than ever.

The man in the lake bobbed to the surface. What was he doing? Tai chi? It looked like an aquatic exercise. Jack would never do such a thing, never submit himself to anything so embarrassing-looking.

Early in the marriage Shana had wanted to become a person of considerable gravity. She read *The Divine Comedy* and *Don Quixote de la Mancha*, *The Travels of Marco Polo* and *Pilgrim's Progress*, *Moll Flanders* and *Candide*, *The Rime of the Ancient Mariner* and *The Tragedy of Faust*, *Pride and Prejudice* and *The Red and the Black*, *The Three Musketeers* and *The Scarlet Letter*, *Camille* and *Moby Dick*, *The Return of the Native* and *The Picture of Dorian Gray*, *The Way of All Flesh* and *Oedipus Rex*, *The Importance of Being Earnest* and *The World as Will and Idea*.

When at last she did what she thought Jack secretly wanted and asked him for a separation, he looked deeply into her eyes. They were in the living room, and for once the television wasn't on to keep them company. At that moment it occurred to Shana that Jack wasn't sympathetic toward her so much as baffled by her. In her turn she was baffled at least as much as he was. She might have been staring into the eyes of a remarkably intelligent garden mole.

"I think," he began, with the note of an adult correcting a child's diction, "you mean a divorce. It's been a mistake. Think about it."

But how could she think when all along the margins of her thoughts lived soft, wounded flesh? At best even now there might be half-healed, half-thickened patches, yet at the center: living, throbbing tissue.

After she left her husband, Shana began working as an assistant to the cultural director—arranging events that were second rate: the sons and daughters of the famous, recreating their parents' careers in an act of rage. Or else she booked in-gratiating singers with decades-old hits behind them. All of them were impersonators of one kind or another, whether they billed themselves as such or not. Some of the men flirted with her, but it was hopeless, their flirtations, and they could be put off by a moment's hesitation.

Anyway, after Jack, how could she trust anyone? When she remembered the way Jack came into her life she could al-most find it in her heart to pity the naïve young woman she had been. They first met in a library while he was skipping out on a pharmaceutical conference to read *Golf Digest*. Even though he was a stranger, he picked up her hand and kissed it. She felt alarm: the act was artificial and out of place. He must have con-fused her with the sort of women who expected such gestures. Like the French. He acted like he won her. From whom? She didn't resist him at all.

The sandy lake bottom sucked at her feet. Shana made herself lie back in the water. She executed a backstroke.

"It's been a mistake," Jack said. "Think about it."

She had assumed he had known himself better. If he wanted her, who was she to prove him wrong? Didn't his experience count for anything? He was so much older than she was. "You're not the first for him by a long shot," her father told her only a week before the wedding. "And I'm afraid you won't be the last by a long shot. He's been married three times. He ought to grow up." She cried that night, wishing she had more memories of her mother, who had died when Shana was five. Everyone who had known Shana's mother said she was an effusive, vibrant woman. At least her mother would have wished her happiness. "You never inherited your mother's good looks," her father let Shana know when she was thirteen. He hadn't spoken disapprovingly.

The man in the water was swimming away from Shana. There was nothing bulky about his shoulders, nothing about him like Jack at all.

For one thing, Jack couldn't swim and never thought of his inability as a failing. He liked dry land and a continual green expanse under bright sun. She never knew how he kept his position in pharmaceuticals, what with all the time he made for golf. Besides, he hated pharmaceuticals. The way he talked you would think drugs were manufactured to create disabilities. Couldn't he quit? she asked. Couldn't he try to change things? He told her she was incapable of understanding his position.

The man in the lake swam toward her. A stream of sunlight lit up his left shoulder before he dove under the water.

Were she and the man alone? Shana looked behind her. Far down the beach, a smudgy group—a family maybe?—were folding up for the afternoon.

When she was eleven Shana's cousins invited her to their cottage on a lake in Michigan. You probably can't even swim, her oldest cousin told her. The cousin was a pretty girl who disdained Shana. Immediately, Shana pretended she knew how to swim, even climbing the diving board. All she had to do was drop to avoid the contempt of her cousin. After Shana entered the water she instantly bounded upward as if drawn to the surface through a straw. For the rest of the afternoon she managed to keep afloat, although her youngest cousin told Shana that her breathing was so scary and loud that she sounded like she was dying.

A more recent memory slid open, and again Shana heard Jack say, "It's been a mistake. Think about it," and she remembered too well what happened next. Shana went to the kitchen and came back into the living room with a glass of iced tea.

She threw the tea into Jack's face, and he struck her across the jaw. Wake up, wake up, wake up, she told herself at that moment. Jack was almost smiling as if he had made a discovery. She was convinced he discovered that he liked her more after he struck her.

The man in the lake did a few neck rolls and catapulted. Would he be bothered that Shana was letting herself float closer to him, and that they were alone together?

The slightest movement she made in the water had repercussions, as if she and the man were in a big bag of jellies. There could be nothing second-rate or shoddy about a man so free with himself and so gentle, yes. He wouldn't hurt her, and she must stop her memories from harming her. She would not be caught forever in her memories. She was a healthy young woman; the scare she had undergone told her that she was all right, after all. Her body had only made a mistake in giving off the wrong signal.

A ripple of water and then another struck her. With each paddling movement, the sight of the man ahead of her grew clearer, almost magnified. His dark bangs were cut straight across his forehead. His eyes were dark.

And then she realized: he couldn't be more than fifteen years old.

She made her feet find the sandy bottom of the lake.

The boy splashily advanced after her.

"Will you be out here tomorrow?" he asked. He touched her shoulder lightly, as if playing tag. His eyelashes were black and thick as a girl's. He might be younger than fifteen.

"My mom and me are staying here for two whole weeks. There's no other kids around. Not my age. Do you have kids?

Not little kids. Somebody my age."

He looked into her eyes as if he expected to find boys there.

He began telling her about his mother and his aunt and how they took him out of summer school and said the experience would be educational. They were going to fit Sea World into the trip. While he spoke, Shana was thinking with shame of how she had made her way toward him through the water so alert to her own potential happiness, so wistful, so ready for life to change in an instant. She'd advanced upon him really. Like a crazed cow moose. How Jack hated her whimsical side.

"What were you doing in the water?" she asked the boy.

"Nothing," he said. He was a good two heads taller than she was.

"But you were doing something," she said. She heard her tone—censorious, as if she knew infinitely more than the boy knew about his own capacities and held him accountable for his ignorance.

The boy's hands flapped to his chest. And then—it was almost funny—he pounded past her, sending spumes of water into the air.

She was sickened by herself. In her own eyes she had taken pleasure in making the boy ashamed for what came naturally to him. Of course she knew what the boy was doing. He was playing.

In the late afternoon Shana and Rachel sat in silence watching the window of their hotel suite stream with rain. None of the scheduled sessions in the main hall or satellite buildings interested them. Rachel blamed their lassitude on what she called "accumulated fatigue" from the plane trip and "that miserable married couple." Shana believed her own lassitude had something to do with mistaking a child for a man.

At first they didn't hear the knock. Later Shana said that it was more like a scratching anyway, as if someone took a small wire brush to the door. Shana wasn't even sure she would find anyone when she opened the door.

"We were hoping you might be in the mood for a drink," Oliver said. Standing before them, the man looked smaller than he had earlier in the day when Shana and Rachel met him and his wife and a party of women who identified themselves as "agents of Social Services" at the breakfast buffet. Shana had noticed Oliver's astonishing smile first. It seemed to come from some source beyond him, running into his eyes in flashes. She didn't expect to see him again, and certainly didn't anticipate that he would find out her suite number. "Connie's in the room with a bucket of ice," he said.

"And gin?" Rachel asked from behind Shana.

"It's almost too cold for a drink, isn't it?" Shana asked tentatively. She was wrapped in a sweater and hugging herself.

"You must have the air conditioning up too high," Oliver said with a whistle. "Connie can make you some hot coffee. We'll even make you some hot Irish coffee. We don't mean to be a nuisance, but this rain calls for an extreme response."

To Shana's surprise, Rachel was the first to give in. "We could stand getting out of our room," she said.

Oliver and Connie's suite must have been the source for the brochure photograph. There were the same blue and yellow interlocking circles on the decor as in Shana and Rachel's room, but the circles were a good three times larger. A kitchenette counter doubled as a bar, behind which stood a full-sized refrigerator.

Oliver fumbled in the refrigerator's depths. Shana, Rachel, and Connie sat on high stools.

As he sliced a lemon Oliver said, "Now tell me, old girl, my dear Rachel—"

Rachel said, "Oliver—may I call you Oliver?—you're making me feel like a horse."

"I'm not capable of it. Now, Shana, however, if you were to tell me that you made me feel like a horse I would take it as a compliment. Wouldn't I, Connie?"

"Don't pay any attention to him," Connie said. "It's the gin. Everyone knows it's a hallucinogen." She looked almost comically nautical, like a diminutive sailor, in her cream-colored blouse with blue piping.

"Is it really?" Shana asked. "I thought it's more like an antidepressant."

"No, no, no," Oliver said. "It starts quarrels that last a lifetime or more. Quarrels that are based on fantasy."

"It ignites grievances," Connie said. "Things you didn't know could bother you start bothering you."

"Especially things that shouldn't bother you," Oliver added.

"And what is it that you're drinking?" Shana asked, turning to Connie. Connie must have been drinking before Shana and Rachel came to the room and now her tall glass was almost empty.

"Juice of the Ram."

"No," Shana gasped, and regretted her gasp. People often wanted to shock her.

"It sounds—what—agricultural?" Connie said.

"At least informed by the rites of animal husbandry," Oliver answered with a clap of laughter. "Don't worry. She's getting me back for earlier calling a concoction I made Fornicating on the Ash Heap. How about this: What if I said that this resort—designed for youth—for maintaining and preserving youth and displaying youth—prematurely ages people?"

"I'd say that you might be right," Rachel said. Shana suspected her friend had been holding her tongue. "But why are you here?" Rachel asked. She was spinning slowly on her stool, catching images: the giant semicircular couch, a partially opened door to a bedroom where the bedspread was loaded with yellow and blue circles.

"I suppose you think that I ought to blather about the reckless consumption that this place mirrors in some strata of our culture," Oliver said, as if he couldn't bother to answer Rachel's question. "Consumption. Reckless, reckless consumption—."

"I hadn't thought about it till now," Connie broke in. "But consumption is the archaic term for tuberculosis, isn't it?"

"Either way it's a wasting disease," Oliver answered her.

No giant waterslides or floating bars were ranged at the side of the pool nearest Shana and Rachel's suite. No Hawaiian lava rocks. The pool nearly qualified as austere—and Shana liked that. She also liked that the lake itself was near, just across one pathway. She could hear the water lapping, and she could try to forgive herself for freaking out that poor boy. She held out the hope that she wouldn't run into him again, although she imagined that it would never occur to him that the mistake was all her own. As if she were channeling Jack and preying on a much younger person. It had been instructive too.

By four o'clock Shana imagined that more people would return to the pool, but except for one small child with an exhausted and whining mother in tow, Shana was alone. The child poked about in the water while her dazed mother watched. Finally, even the child couldn't resist her mother's urging that they go to the lounge for lemonades.

Shana rose from the pool to read her magazine in the shade of shrubs and potted trees. Her arms and legs felt limp, as if the water had somehow gotten under her skin, weakening her.

She woke to darkness and laughter. She swung her legs from the chaise lounge and scooted forward. Nets of shadow and light reflected from the lit torches.

She was surprised to see Oliver in the pool. There was so much boiling in the water around him—splashing and laughter. Women were surrounding him but not, apparently, paying attention to him.

"You bet!" Oliver said too loudly, and Shana winced for him. An older, needy man, incautious enough to reveal himself. There was more commotion in the water. The women were a rowdy bunch, and soon Oliver pulled himself out of the pool. His limbs were short and nearly hairless. He settled onto a low-backed chair.

One after another, the women rose from the pool, shaking themselves and grabbing towels. The last woman out of the water—a thick blonde with black roots whom Shana had seen the first morning at the brunch—pushed a button at the edge of the pool to turn on the spa while the other women were on their way toward the glass doors that led to the showers. Oliver was motionless, unacknowledged in his chair, his head tipped back. And then the blonde woman with dark roots walked up to Oliver, straddled his chair, and lowered herself over him.

How could Shana leave without being seen? She would have to back out and walk on the path beside the lake, as if she were the one who should be embarrassed.

The luau was set up on the grounds of the not-quite-completed Health Top Inn. A cherry picker partially blocked the inn's front façade, but at the far rear, away from the traffic cones, an ornamental bridge spanned a mock lagoon. Tables were arranged on the flagstones and a stage was erected past the umbrella chairs and potted palms. The boy from the lake was nowhere in evidence.

"Is this your first luau?" Oliver asked. He put his hand on Shana's shoulder. She flinched.

"I'm sorry," he said.

Shana apologized in turn. "My nerves," she said.

His hand didn't move. From opposite her, Shana could feel Rachel's disapproval.

"I suppose you've had your share of luaus," Oliver said to Rachel.

"No, it's actually only my second one ever. I've been looking for the luau pig. You wouldn't know his whereabouts?" Her tone was so withering that Shana froze.

Oliver took his hand from Shana's shoulder, excused himself, and headed toward Connie, seated several tables away.

Shana could feel his hand on her shoulder still. Did Oliver know she had seen him at the pool last night? But what was she supposed to do? Shout out the substance of last night to Connie? And what had she witnessed? Maybe her eyes were fooling her. For all she knew, Oliver dumped the woman on the pool mat after she straddled him.

"Shana and Rachel must think we're following them," Connie said, when the women unavoidably—a small crowd was forming behind them in the buffet line and pressing Shana and

Rachel forward—wound up near Connie and Oliver's table. "I'm not stalking you," Connie went on. "But apparently Oliver is. Of course he stalks everybody, so none of us can flatter ourselves."

Oliver laughed and stood. "It's only a wonderful coincidence," he said. "But I do hope that we're all good friends. Stay a little while. If you had the seven dwarves for your own, what tasks would you allot them?"

"Yes, please, sit down. This is Oliver's favorite game," Connie said.

Shana was flooded with sympathy for Connie—and confusion. If she didn't accept Oliver's invitation, Shana felt that in some obscure way she would be hurting Connie, as if Connie needed her. Shana gathered her strength—the way she did whenever some new act came to the cultural center, some new set of brittle egos.

"Oh no. Do our answers constitute a secret autobiography?" she asked. She accepted the chair Oliver offered, setting down her tray. "Well, my favorite is Doc. I guess it makes him sound like he has a medical degree. But you have to wonder about all of them. In Disney, they have names on their beds. So they don't forget who they are—"

"And get into the wrong bed," Connie said.

How creepy, Shana thought. Still, she tried to normalize the conversation. "They don't look like they're related, do they?" she said. She told herself that soon she'd never have to see this couple ever again.

"Wasn't there a dwarf named Gruesome?" Rachel asked.

"Ah—we love you," Oliver said, raising his glass. He looked as if he knew the dwarves were getting nowhere, especially with Rachel. He turned to Shana. "Do you think of your body as a project?" he asked.

Shana looked at Oliver uncomprehendingly.

"Answer me truthfully," Oliver said. "So what is it? Do you think of your amazing, unforgettable body as a project?"

"Why are you being so invasive with Shana?" Rachel said.

"I think you're misinterpreting an innocent question. I was only trying to be attentive. Projects. We all have goals."

"I'm not interested in projects," Shana said. "I'm on vacation."

"Oliver, I want you to answer Rachel's question," Connie said. "Why are you troubling Shana?"

"I'm hoping for some sort of response. I'm getting agitated by the number of people here who treat their bodies like projects. Like paint-by-number kits. I'm only asking for a fresh point of view. It's ugly—the way people treat their bodies."

"And this depresses you?" Connie asked.

"It doesn't depress you?"

"No. It reveals a certain amount of practicality," Connie said. "The body is the one area where people can have some control."

"You would think the sheer number of treatments here—mud, milk, massage—" Shana began.

"You've got the m's down," Oliver said.

Shana tried again. "You'd think the treatments would make everybody look like walking bruises. Except for maybe the salt baths. Acupuncture all over the place. People getting plugged full of holes."

Connie and Oliver exchanged a glance and laughed. Shana felt it in the air—some agreement had been made between them.

"God, I love morbidity," Oliver said. "I knew we'd all get along. Except for Rachel. You can't stand me, Rachel, can you?"

Shana's impulse was to stand up and leave, but Rachel wasn't moving. It was almost as if Rachel wasn't listening at all. But then, she was from a large family. She probably had a lot of practice ignoring people.

"That's one of the mysteries," Oliver said. "Instant antipathy."

"Oliver has that effect," Connie said. "I wanted to murder him after I first met him. It took me about five minutes to decide he ought to be destroyed."

"Like a rabid dog," Oliver said.

"Yes, you ought to be put down," Connie answered him.

"If Rachel would give me a chance—" Oliver said.

"Really, Oliver," Connie interrupted. "There's hardly time for a chance. Why should she spend her vacation catering to an imperfect stranger?"

"You're right. As always. Thank goodness Shana at least tolerates me."

Shana was rescued by steel guitars. On the stage near the potted palms a woman in a bushy skirt turned in a spotlight. "Ouch," Oliver said. "Ouch." He thrust his head forward and backward as if the rotations on stage were aimed at him. Shana felt such intense irritation that she pushed her chair back. But now Rachel was gone—nowhere in sight. Rachel was only interested in her own escape. She hadn't even signaled Shana, as if Shana could take care of herself. And of course I can, Shana thought.

She looked at the nearby tables for the boy from the lake and felt almost giddy relief that she didn't see his innocent face again. She probably should apologize to him. She should tell him that she didn't mean to make him unhappy, that it was a mistake. But then, he was so young he wouldn't know what she was talking about. He wouldn't even know why he had suddenly been scared and got out of the water. He had good instincts. Anyway, why hadn't she discovered rum earlier in her life? Who first discovered rum? Or could you really discover rum? Wasn't it more like an invention? The rum she was drinking was remarkable. No, it was more than remarkable. It was marvelous—as if you could distill the garden of Eden, all those flowers and fruits.

At some point Connie left, silently, except for leaving a pyramid of money, enough for all their drinks and a tip. Wasn't Connie always to be in attendance? Wasn't she Oliver's handler? Weren't Oliver and Connie the most artificial couple Shana had ever met? Some of the most unwholesome people?

"Oh, darling, nothing to fear from me," Oliver said, as if reading her thoughts came naturally to him. He smiled a full, breath-taking smile. "Stay here with me for about twenty more minutes," he said. "Just enough to keep Connie waiting."

"She leaves you alone with women you hardly know? Is that an agreement between you?"

"Now that you mention it, it should be. I ought to negotiate for the right to be left alone to have rum punch with young girls and then make them want to crouch in the bushes with me. The instant I laid eyes on you I told Connie: she's the one."

"The one what?"

"The right one."

The morning sunlight was sweeping away all evidence of a light rain. The courtyard was alive with rustlings in the miniature palms. Shana and Rachel were sitting on the balcony outside their suite. Shana told herself that last night was nothing she would ever enter into again.

She remembered images most—the flash of the bedroom as she stumbled out of the suite, and Connie looking old and wizened in an aqua nightgown, her legs folded under her. And Oliver, his withered face hanging upside down.

"Was it sickening?" Rachel asked. "It had to be sickening."

"I don't know what you mean."

"They probably didn't even give us their real names. But it's your life," Rachel said. "Did they ask you what dwarf you wanted to be?"

"We didn't get that far."

Shana could see it again: Connie on the lumpy bed and more drinks on a table and then Shana saw herself as if she hovered above her own body: she was vomiting on the rug's circles. Then she saw her head plunging against the carpet and then she saw thick yellow carpet fibers. Oliver's hands were on her waist. He wanted to move her into another room, but Shana was trying to stand, and stumbling, swinging her arms, pushing him away and lurching out the door and through the corridor to the exit and down the shrub-lined path before she made herself stop, the dawn spinning around her. It took all her effort to stay on her feet, as if she were leaning over a cliff. She heard a padding sound behind her. A jogger passed in a sizzle of nylon—too close—almost brushing her shoulder.

Below Shana and Rachel's balcony a couple were already soaking in the whirlpool. They lifted themselves out of the water, both of them pink and steaming, the color of shrimp, with tattoos on their legs, at the upper thigh of each, at her right thigh, his left.

"My little brother—the youngest, the one you met last month—called last night," Rachel said. "He can't wait till we get home. He kept asking about you."

Shana was glad that they would be going soon—glad to leave their suite, which was cramped with its small, fussy circles on the wallpaper and the rugs and the bedspreads. She wanted to have time to think, and she could think better when she was alone.

So far she had arrived at only a few conclusions: what some people wanted was for other people to stop thinking. People like that imagined you were just like them, that you understood that they were proposing a game and that you were in on the game. That's how everything started: people believed you were playing a game like their game and punished you for ruining the game, or else you learned how to punish yourself for them.

Nevertheless, there was some lesson she kept avoiding or missing. She just had to be careful. And no more pretending.

No more pretending to feel something when she didn't.

No more pretending not to feel something when she did.

No more pretending to be helpless, witless, accommodating, eager, small, young.

The Undressed Mirror

An actor is an undressed mirror
reflecting an audience's light.
The audience must never know
the mirror is what they see—
and that is why the mirror rises before them undressed
as an ordinary creature of
ordinary flesh,
yet casting silver light.
                    —Yanis Karlotz, trans. by Eavan Liss

I hadn't been able to renew the lease on my apartment, and
that was the least of it. It was a miracle when Jocelyn called and
asked if I would watch over The Blue Oyster while she was in
Ghana for three weeks. The hotel would be closed during her
absence, but she still needed a caretaker. The woman Jocelyn
had hired for the purpose bailed.

All this was arranged over the phone. Jocelyn's warnings
and recommendations grew so complex that I began taking notes.
I wished then that I could talk about the entire situation with
my mother. I still regularly have the urge to phone her until I
remember. No calling her. No hearing that voice ever again.

Had Jocelyn known she was saving me? When I was a kid
I seldom entered Jocelyn's quarters behind The Blue Oyster's
reception desk—not into the tiny rooms dank with humidity,

including the miniature kitchen. Instead I spent a lot of time in the foyer where Jocelyn and my mother drank vodka with lime and reminisced until they bored my brother Robin and me, while hotel guests came and went.

And now I was, once again, after all those years, looking around the foyer, relieved that I had somewhere to live and wouldn't hear over the phone Robin's relentless stock advice and my sister-in-law's nervous questions. Everything in the foyer looked eerily preserved: the dried pampas grass in jade urns, the mahogany buffet, the liver-colored marble fireplace shadowed with decades of soot. Even the afghans on the foyer couches were the same as I remembered, except that their orange yarn was faded to pale sherbet.

I was the changed one. No more stage work. No more even trying to call myself an actress. Eamon used to correct me: *You're an actor. Say actor, not actress.* I never minded being called an actress. *It rhymes with distress, progress, regress, undress*, I told Eamon.

I had been lucky in actors, Eamon being my favorite. I had almost worked as well with Esther Wilno-Medi who could unfreeze most actors, thaw and remold instincts—who even turned a switch on Paulie Matheres, who went on to survive on standup comedy alone. But in the end neither Esther nor Eamon could work magic for me.

It was Eamon who had to walk me offstage, Eamon who took my arm and drew me away when I was unable to speak another word in the second act of a play that should not have given me any trouble whatsoever.

One of the tasks I set myself at Jocelyn's hotel: cleaning out the lost and found room. Fifteen years of accumulated junk.

Jocelyn asked me to keep anything I liked but to give away the rest or to dispose of what couldn't be saved. In the first box I pulled out five hooded jackets and three negligees with butterflies, twelve socks, and at least twenty pornographic magazines. Within four hours I had cleaned only half of the room—enough to fill twelve boxes for the Clauden Charities, ahead of the annual jumble sale advertised in the bulletin that turned up on the hotel's doorstep that morning.

After another half hour of sorting I was making quicker progress when, at the bottom of a collapsed cardboard box, a filmy square of cloth slipped between my fingers. I shook the fabric into the light. A dress, its fabric so fine it could have been spun from thistledown. The stitching looked done by hand, and the material smelled faintly of lavender. *You were lost and now you're found, you beautiful thing.*

I hung the dress behind the door of my room where in a draft the featherlight fabric rose like a pale Titania.

"Are you in your car?" I asked.

Eamon's phone gave out an eerie echo. "No. I'm at home. With soup. Maybe you're hearing me eat soup?" I thought of the astonishingly limber way Eamon could cross a stage on his knees. That night he would be in another dinner-theater mystery beneath his talents. There were pirates. "Yesterday, someone—five minutes in—shouted, correctly, that my character was the murderer," he said. "No one believed her. Plus, we changed the ending. At intermission we had Amanda Watts ad lib a confession. It made no sense, but everyone loved it. Amanda most of all."

His voice sounded strange before he finished talking, as if he regretted mentioning anything connected to acting. Not for the first time the thought occurred: for how long would Eamon respect me? We had worked together in drafty former barns, the wooden beams above us pitted by termites, dust burning in our throats. *Caspar's Wedding* was enough to make me believe we'd pressed a lifetime of quarrels, heartache, stupefaction, and panic into one run-through. And in *A Midsummer Night's Dream* as Demetrius he had spurned me as an addled Helena ("I am your spaniel"). I had loved the role—the desperate, lovesick woman, willing to betray even her closest friend for a man who didn't want her. As far as women are concerned, the play should be a tragedy. But Eamon—my deepest friend in the art—what did he think of me now? How long could he keep on, kindly dealing with what I had become when it was incomprehensible to us both?

I asked him what else he was working on, and when he spoke again his voice relaxed. "I'm resurrecting 'The Undressed Mirror.' A ten-minute piece. You remember—it's based on that poem about actors being undressed mirrors."

"Instead of undressed people."

"I'm working on a few things, but I don't want to give up on, you know, nakedness of any sort."

"Have you seen Sofie's movie?" I asked.

"I don't think it's opened yet. And I don't think she's working right now. That can be dangerous."

"Her last movie—she did well with that," I said. "At least it opened in theaters."

"She won't be in the sequel unless they raise the dead. But at least there's this new movie. I'm looking forward to that. She told me she's going to invite herself over to the hotel. She's probably the last thing you need."

It was then that I asked the question: "Eamon, what was

it like for you?"

"What was what like?"

"When you had to take me off the stage. Audry Alains said I looked like a 'leftover zombie.' That's a direct quote. What did it look like to you?"

It was impossible for me to understand what happened when Eamon led me away while the audience applauded out of pity and confusion. And I could not understand why it happened again the next night. And then the next. After that I wouldn't allow anyone to talk me into performing again.

The phone was full of windy spaces. Eamon hesitated before he said, "Do you remember that Christopher Durang play *The Actor's Nightmare*? The guy thinks he's in *Hamlet* then he's in—what?—*Blithe Spirit*?—maybe. Then it's *A Man for All Seasons*—and then the actor is beheaded and can't take his curtain call? Claire, you turned the evening experimental. As for that zombie description by Audry. It doesn't work. Except: remember this: remember, zombies are popular. Really popular. They'll never not be popular. Just blow through it. Listen. You must have looked great to the audience. A total emptying out of personality and will. You were like a statue there—and a lot of people must have thought it was just part of the play. Galatea turning back into marble or something."

I could hear him breathe again. Trying to breathe for me.

Sofie attempted to call me while I was talking to Eamon. She left a message: "Don't tell me there's no room at the inn. Not when you live in a hotel. I'm not sure what time of day I'll get there or when. I'll let you know—soon. Hah! Very soon. Don't worry. About entertaining me. I'll entertain myself. I certainly can't entertain anyone else these days. When it opens be

Lee Upton

sure to skip my movie, promise? It's eerie and stupid. It will bore you. Skip it. Promise me you'll skip it. Speaking of eerie, you're aware that I'm coming to cheer you up, right? So we'll see each other in Clauden—at last." It was a long message and it wasn't over. She began recounting her week's schedule, which involved three consecutive parties with actors we both had worked with.

When I called her back, Sofie said, "Your life sounds like *The Shining* meets *Nights at Rodanthe*. Or like one of Eamon's plays. Have you heard about his Alfred Hitchcock comedy? With a chorus."

"I thought it was about a woman in a haunted hotel."

"He's not going to profit from your freaky situation. His play's haunted by Hitchcock's movies. Not the crappy ones. He's not going to put anyone through *Topaz*. It's a collage— montage—whatever. There's some *Rear Window* sampling. It's like this giant apartment complex, and there's the *Marnie* window with this superheated sexually suggestive scene. A nude fox chase. He needs more of those. And then there's the *Vertigo* window where people keep falling off stepladders. It's a fantasia on suspense. I bet that in Eamon's fantasies you'd work with Hitchcock. You'd be perfect. Like Tippi Hedren. Not Kim Novak. Even less like Eva Marie Saint."

"I'm not blonde."

"You could become blonde. So you're a woman alone in a hotel. You don't have to identify with Janet Leigh." She cleared her throat, and I braced myself. Even over the phone it was always evident when something I didn't want to hear would come from Sofie: "Claire, you never laugh much anymore. You used to be so wild, so funny. That's gone—almost all of it. I won't mention it again. I just thought you should know. As for Eamon's play. He sent me a copy. I have a few lines you could try out."

I worked to steady my voice. "I feel less like laughing by the minute. Are you going to have me say the lines from Eamon's play to prove I can do it? Is that what this is about?"

"You're too self-involved, Claire. This is about me."

"Okay. See. You've made me laugh. About Eamon's play—I bet there's a lot of subtext."

"He prefers the word *obsession*. Eamon should write a new part for you. Just remember, stage fright affects the best actors, especially the top rank. Richard Burton—he always wore red for it—although why that would help I can't think. Red. If red helped I'd tattoo my own ass red. Laurence Olivier. Scared to death before going onstage. He always seemed like such a prick. He probably spread the story to make himself more likable. What I'm trying to say is: you're not alone with what happened to you. You're not the only one who gets stage fright."

"But I wasn't afraid."

Who could have warned me about the way mourning works and how it doesn't ever quite end? There are so many after-effects. Aching heaviness in your arms, exactly as if you're lifting something heavy that's invisible. Buzzing inside your fingertips, as if you almost touched an electrified fence. Then those moments of forgetfulness until you're brought short by a reminder.

How did anyone deal with it? There was Arian Roth who said she would never recover after her mother's death, who spoke as if her heart were torn into strips. At the opposite extreme: Gunter Pohl who despised his mother so vocally that his friends questioned after her death if they should offer condolences. Or Gwynne Tweedy with her "death is just a part of life" mantra, although she'd had a reasonably good relationship with her mother. Before my own mother's death I had listened to Gwynne and thought, "No, it's not a part of life. That's why it's called death."

Sofie knew of my mother's death, and yet it didn't occur to her that I was still in mourning. Nor did Sofie know—no one knew—of my discovery of a small immaculate truth among the papers I sorted after my mother's death. Through those papers I learned that, a month after I was born, my mother gave me away. Seven weeks later she reclaimed me from the family who had expected to adopt me. I couldn't imagine the scene or my mother's reasoning. She wasn't married, but poverty wasn't the problem. She hadn't really been concerned about her reputation either—that wasn't in her character. Was she sick and unable to take care of me? Had she wanted another sort of child? Had she been disappointed in me? Why was I never told the truth?

Then again, when would be the right time for a mother to tell her daughter she gave her away—even though she reclaimed her? And now, why should it bother me at all? Had the discovery stopped me onstage—the one place I had aimed my life toward? I didn't think so. In fact, I believed that such a simple explanation couldn't account for what had happened. There had to be a less obvious reason. Maybe I would never know what stopped me from acting. And that was horrible. Not knowing. Not being able to trust myself. And having no explanation, no way to get at the root of the truth.

A flash of sunlight dropped from the clouds. Eamon was driving, and we were winding along the Sirreque River, between the canal and a cliff where ferns gushed between rocks.

"Where exactly are you taking me?"

"A surprise. You need a good surprise. You're exhausted, aren't you?"

"I shouldn't be. I'm not doing anything. I vacuum the place. I answer the doorbell for repairmen. I cleaned out the lost and found room—which turned out to be a depository for pornography through the decades. Other than that I'm not doing anything. Doing nothing is really tiring."

When I opened my eyes again, Eamon said, "There's something I want to show you." He pulled into a vacant lot, drove through an alley, and parked the car at the rear of a brick building. Only two high windows were visible near the roofline. "It's not much," he said, "but it's worth imagining the prospects."

I knew what the interior of the building would look like: dusty velvet curtains, a wooden ticket booth near the entrance, framed theater programs. And I knew what Eamon was thinking: that I was almost ready to return to being the person I had been, that whatever was holding me back could be conquered, that staying at the hotel had allowed me time to recuperate— all those things I had hoped for too.

At last Eamon said, "I'm an idiot. I'm sorry."

My throat was tightening with shame.

Eamon tried again. "Claire. Listen. Was it the lights?"

I didn't know what he was talking about. He went on, "I've been thinking. The lights were on you when you had to stop. In rehearsals we didn't have the lights working—not even during dress rehearsal. Remember? There was a problem. With the light board."

We sat together in silence. Finally I said, "The lights?"

It was while I was in a drama called *Mercury's Wonder* that I had to stop acting. Through every rehearsal the playwright was in attendance, his mouth open with astonishment. There was something both repulsive and gratifying about seeing him there. He was a sensitive guy who lost weight so rapidly that three members of the cast brought in trail mix and bananas for him. He declined everything but coffee and kept assuring me that he loved my interpretation of my character. I had the suspicion that, as long as the words he wrote were spoken clearly, he would have loved anyone's interpretation. Two days before the opening I discovered the incriminating papers about my near-adoption.

It was a ridiculous play. Nihilistic too. The third act setting: a dumpster. Beckett would have wept hot silly tears. Sofie showed up during dress rehearsal and kept shaking her head to the point that I noticed her during my monologue and had to strangle a bark of laughter. Afterwards, she voiced her opinion: "That play created suffering. If you want people to suffer you have to really make them suffer. But why you want them to suffer is beyond me. People are numb from suffering. The guy who wrote that play had the emotional life of a totalitarian douche." Then, softening, she said, "You were great, Claire. Without you, that play would go nowhere. Although it really wants to go nowhere. I really admire your persistence. You never give up."

The next night I went into my first standing coma halfway through my monologue. I almost wanted to blame Sofie.

It would be a quiet little party. Not a costume party. So many of my friends had costume parties. *Come As You Were Born*—that was a good party. A woman with the spectacular name Connie Trash came wrapped in cellophane with a string licorice umbilical cord. *The Turn of the Screw* party—another good one. Although too many slutty governesses and feeble attempts at impersonating hardware. No, those sorts of parties wouldn't work among the few people I knew in Clauden. Besides, I couldn't help myself: I was interested in Jocelyn's realtor,

Matthew Elmwhist, a widower and the father of a little girl that I was already falling in love with. I met Matthew when I went to pick up the keys to the hotel at his office. I saw him and his little girl the next day at the grocery store. I felt so much inexplicable tenderness for them both that I couldn't resist telling Eamon and Sofie about them.

The party seemed like a way to get to know Matthew and also a way to give myself something to look forward to. It was a way, too, for me to convince Jocelyn, when she returned, that I had been trying to make some friends, to be less isolated. It was obvious what Jocelyn wanted for me: a rest cure and a prolonged distraction, as if my trouble—my inability to act onstage, the thoughts that plagued me—came about through overexhaustion, overstimulation. As if I had pushed my mind too far, as if a mind is a piece of heavy furniture that can't be shoved without ruining the floorboards.

The next afternoon I invited the mail carrier and two of the women at the deli to the party. It was anticipation of the party that was carrying me through the hours.

The night before the party, a taxi driver, dreadlocked and with oatmeal-colored skin, arrived to deposit Sofie at the hotel. When I hugged her she felt skinnier than ever. Almost childlike, her spine knobby as if set with beads.

She stepped back and her voice rose. "How do you like it? My hair. I was aiming for Karen Black in the Robert Redford *Gatsby*—in that scene where she gets Bruce Dern to buy her a puppy."

In the foyer I announced "I can give you the deluxe suite. Plus, there are doilies."

"That settles it."

"And yellow wallpaper."

She laughed. "I once played that woman, that crazy woman, in a production of *The Yellow Wallpaper*? Albany. I had to crawl around the stage scratching walls. Like I was clawing at the audience. There were titters. At my madness. Now for serious matters. What will you wear to this party you're surprising me with?"

"I hadn't thought that far."

At dinner that night she said she'd been sleep-deprived for weeks. Nevertheless, an hour after she said she was going to bed she came into my room. She was wearing pajamas with giant circles on them, like red blood cells. Her eyelashes were almost colorless. Without makeup she looked years younger.

"Let's trade clothes for the party," she said.

"I couldn't squeeze into anything you wear."

"I haven't lost weight."

I looked at her doubtfully. "Maybe I've gained." Then I remembered the dress from the lost and found room and showed it to her.

"It's yours," I said. "To keep. Please."

"Are you serious?"

The dress, unbelievably soft and light, stirred as I handed it over.

"It really is beautiful. But you should keep it," Sofie said. "It's gorgeous."

"It's for you. It is you."

Three years earlier I was in a tribute to Virginia Woolf in which Enid Castrova played a remarkable Mrs. Dalloway. The atmosphere on opening night made it seem like we were at an enchanted party, as if a breeze blew across the stage after a storm, as if anything could happen and whatever happened would shimmer. My own heart was thumping with exhilaration throughout the whole second act.

If only my party at Jocelyn's hotel could have been like that party.

Within a half hour, Eamon was wearing an expression that I recognized. I had seen him like that onstage—whenever he wished he were in another play.

Sofie kept twitching as if the dress I gave her itched.

Maybe I should have invited more people to the party, although that would have meant meeting more people in Clauden previous to the party, and I hadn't. I was relieved that Matthew came, but I felt shy in his presence. He was even taller than I remembered and at first he hardly looked at me. Sofie didn't speak a word to Matthew after I introduced him and stayed out of his way every time he passed the buffet.

But then Matthew seemed to loosen up, and soon he laughed at all of Eamon's jokes. I liked him even more for laughing at Eamon's jokes. Then I asked him about his little girl. She was staying with his aunt for the night. We talked about her for a while. She loved zebras, and I remembered that there were some wonderful stuffed animals at a little store I'd seen just the past weekend. I was beginning almost to feel hope for the party.

Eamon leaned close to Sofie and said, "Do you remember that one act I did at Simon's Cabaret?"

She shook her head.

"*The Catcher's Mitt*? The history of baseball in three innings? It's being revived."

I couldn't hear Sofie's response. She left the foyer. Every fifteen minutes or so she kept disappearing, either into her room or into the hotel's tiny kitchen area.

Lee Upton

It was another hour before the arrival of a bartender—someone that Jocelyn had insisted I get in touch with when she first contacted me. He had popped in through the rear exit. He worked just a block away from the hotel and was holding a bottle of rum aloft. I waved Sofie over to introduce them to each other. That's when Sofie drew herself up, pressing her shoulders back. The zone around her changed—and for a few seconds whatever it was, this powerful emanation, this magnetic field—materialized before evaporating. For the first time it occurred to me: she was not always a strong actress, but through an effort of will alone she could always make herself into a brilliant presence. At the same time I felt a sense of familiarity—as if I'd seen Sofie like this before—or else I'd seen someone else do exactly this same thing. It also occurred to me that something about her that night was no more believable when it came to showing genuine emotion than the Easter Bunny. Or maybe it was more like watching a magic act. But Sofie would say: what's wrong with a magic act? And I had to admit: it was a gift, what Sofie practices, and a gift should never be underestimated.

When Eamon was leaving I followed him outside. In the darkness he knocked over a shovel on the porch. He jumped around on one foot and made a mock face of such exquisite pain that I laughed. Watching him drive away I remembered what it was like being in a show with him, that sensation of total immersion and expansion. Like swimming underwater without even needing to breathe. The sensation of loss was so fierce that I couldn't let anyone see my face for a while.

When I went back inside, the woman from the deli was ready to leave and wanted her sweater. I went into the first room off the foyer to retrieve it for her, and that's when I saw Matthew and Sofie. I walked backward out of the room. I remembered then that I hadn't put the sweater in the bedroom anyway but had put it in Jocelyn's service closet.

It's not that I saw anything in that room off the foyer that should have surprised me. It's just that what I had seen earlier when Sofie met the bartender was a case of misdirection.

When Sofie and Matthew emerged into the foyer again I could hardly look at either of them. I was glad that Matthew was leaving, although I remembered my first sight of his little daughter buttoned into a red coatlike dress that hung down to her ankles—she was a tiny colorful Cossack—and my heart lurched.

Later that night it would occur to me that if I were in a play or a movie by this point the audience would expect me eventually to find true love with Matthew—after complications. His height alone would be an indication of future possibilities.

I startled when Sofie wandered into the kitchen the next morning, saying she needed to head back to the city for an audition. She hadn't mentioned anything about that earlier.

"You kept leaving the foyer during the party," I said. "Was anything wrong? It wasn't much of a party, I admit."

"Leaving a room isn't my problem. I ought to leave more rooms regularly."

"He's an interesting guy," I said. "He has a little girl. She's—."

"I know."

Being an actor—it's like being an amnesiac. You have to forget each previous role. You're this new person with a new set of complications, possibly even a new accent, certainly a new cadence, a new chord of harmony or disharmony, a shift in vibration. You have to drown that last person you were, or shove her into a back room. I could at least do that—I could forget quite well, at least certain things.

After Sofie left I was getting something from my room when the dress I thought I had given to her fell from a hanger behind the door. A soft sound, like snowmelt.

Every face has hot spots that the camera reveals. Every face has a particular quality, a way of catching and releasing light on a movie screen. But it's always a shock to see someone you know in a movie.

The thing is: you start superimposing the face you know with this mammoth face that appears before you like a hallucination. The first time I saw Sofie on the screen it was like watching a gold balloon being blown up. And then, little by little, she became human, and someone else: a woman lying on a cruise ship deckchair, until a man—an English actor I once met at a bar and briefly flirted with—ambled up.

That first movie's main attraction wasn't any of the actors. It was an eel, a giant eel. And it was obvious that by the end of the movie—a movie ludicrous even by industry standards—the eel would destroy everyone but the best-known actress. Sofie hadn't given details, and so I couldn't guess when she would die.

It was not just because Sofie was my friend, it was not for those reasons that as scenes flashed by I began to be disturbed when I watched her in her first movie. The problem was most evident when the soundtrack cued up. The emotions that passed over Sofie's face never quite fit the words. The part that killed me: when Sofie's face broke into a smile right as she was being swallowed. The inside of the eel's mouth looked slick, like wet black plastic. It was as if Sofie had been shoved into a giant garbage bag. Smiling as she disappeared.

I was surprised the cut even made it. Sofie looked like she was enjoying everything—although the scene went by so quickly and in such fragments that I was left with a cold impression more than an acute certainty the first time I watched it.

The new movie would show a different side of my friend's talent, given that it was based on an obscure novel by Turvet Juvvaor, a near Nobel winner who never fails to write about panic-driven women in quietly sinister situations. A year ago I had read the slim little novel the film was based on. All the dramatic action occurred in the crevices of the novel. It's hard to imagine how a film could be made from that sort of plotless fiction. The producers must have been banking on a star: Ingrid Permulutter.

Three teenage boys trundled into the theater and slumped into seats a couple rows ahead of me. After even more previews than usual, the movie began.

A gray sky. A canal. A dead pigeon. Cathedral spires. The interior of a mosque. A claustrophobic, sterile, urban apartment with a glass coffee table. I was longing to see a human being when at last the majestic Ingrid Permulutter wafted across the screen, apparently playing a woman a whole lot like the majestic Ingrid Permulutter. She was in the apartment and soulfully listening to piano music wafting in from some other apartment while she cut onions. There was a close-up of a cutting board. Shadows at the window. The canal. Another dead pigeon. By that point I wondered if the three teenagers would leave the theater. No. They were texting.

It was a good fifteen minutes until—seen initially as a reflection in a window—Sofie appeared. Slowly her character brought a book to Permulutter. A shot of both women's hands. Then the two women sat by a window, reading, huddled close. Somehow the effect was vaguely unsettling, as if violence threatened just outside the frame.

Bizarrely, the film was like the novel. Except maybe there were nude scenes? Why else would the boys be in the theater unless someone promised them nude scenes? Ingrid Permulutter was known for nude scenes. But the lighting was vaguely gray and blue. Her nude body would look like raw hamburger in that lighting.

Ingrid Permulutter began talking about a tractor. I'm serious.

Nevertheless, something unblocked in me. Maybe it happened because I was relaxing into the horribleness of the movie. Maybe I was feeling vaguely superior. But then—without meaning to—I was within the consciousness on the screen, behind Ingrid Permulutter's eyes. It was like melting into another dimension, and I wasn't aware of myself or of what I'd lost. It was a precious, wonderful thing. It was the closest I'd felt to acting since I left the theater.

By the time I could bring myself back to what was actually occurring on the screen, another friend of Permulutter's character arrived, a big-chested bushily-bearded man with a pony tail like a brillo pad who looked ready to scold Permulutter and Sofie's characters for something or other. I was losing the plot, losing everything, and then I began watching my friend in the corner of the screen, watching the way Sofie turned her head, brushed her hair from her face, laughed.

My skin knew first. That's where the crawling sensation

started. I began telling myself I was making a mistake. Until I was certain. What I was watching in Sofie's character was laughable, needy, raw. She was playing a woman without skin, without the most basic mask. Sofie had used me—had built her character out of my gestures, the way I pushed my hair back from my forehead, the way I crossed my legs, the way I sighed and looked at the ceiling when I was trying to hide my feelings, the way I pronounced consonants that have always given me trouble, the nervous tics that even I recognize as my own.

It was as if I was watching myself being slowly skinned alive. Sofie was putting on my skin. And there was nothing I could do. I told myself not to sensationalize what I was seeing, but it was like watching a murder when I was the woman being murdered on the screen.

One of the teenage boys laughed stupidly. It was an imitation of my most nervous laugh. He'd heard the laugh from Sofie's mouth.

The next morning waves blasted the sand, leaving behind a watery sheen fine as the cataract of an eye. The water was still too cold for swimming.

When I was a young girl we always arrived at the hotel in full summer. I had loved standing in the surf, the waves washing around me like scald on milk. I would run to the hotel, dripping wet, sand in my hair. By the time I got to the hotel's steps the sun would have warmed my back and dried me off.

Back then my mother once told Robin and me that God creates no duplicates. For proof she said that every fingerprint is individual. To which Robin, mature even as a seven-year-old, had asked, "How do you know they're all different? Do they have everybody's fingerprints?"

I had been comforted by my mother's reasoning, which seemed to suggest something about the soul.

Did Sofie impersonate me just because she was so good at it? Was that her art: impersonation? There it was: a woman I trusted had betrayed me at a level I didn't have words for.

Had Eamon seen the movie yet? Eamon would be objective. He would think—as I did, reluctantly, that it was the best work Sophie had ever done.

Two days before Jocelyn was due to return I found myself pulling my car off behind the abandoned theater Eamon had driven me to see. The building loomed large and faceless in the twilight. I hesitated a long time before I got out of my car. Once I did, I could hear a stream churning from somewhere behind the building. I walked toward the sound.

The twilight was deepening. Leaves hung thickly in the trees, heaving as if sopping with rain. With each step I needed to draw sticky cobwebs away from my face and hair. With a low swishing like the sound of a dress against a woman's legs, reeds scissored on the creek bank. And then wonderfully enough: light bounced between the shrubs and trees—gold flickers. The first fireflies. I had never seen so many.

I imagined *A Midsummer Night's Dream* staged right there, in the open, behind the abandoned theater. I could almost hear broken rhythms—like birdsong or traffic in the distance—not the individual lines I'd memorized from dozens of plays, but a sort of mingled music from all of them, as if the sounds were traveling from my earlier life. After a curtain call the echoes of voices from onstage didn't stop but only faded until I slowly returned to my regular life, folding back into being the person I knew myself as: *So this is who I am—this is my life. This odd, funny, precious, arbitrary life.* It used to take me forever to get to sleep after a show. I was overwhelmed by the spreading warmth of a certain sort of faith, the belief that I had doubled my time on earth by inhabiting another sensibility.

Did I go too far in imagining that what Eamon and Sofie and I did enhanced life and lessened the quantity of grief in every audience? Did we allow people to forget, to move beyond what they had been, to lose themselves the same way that we lost ourselves onstage? What an ambitious woman I had been—back when I had known that there are unfathomable possibilities, and that any life has to be reclaimed again and again.

What Sofie had done: she had made me into a caricature to myself and to anyone who knew me. I suppose that if a mere acquaintance had done the same it wouldn't have made such a difference. But a stranger wouldn't have known how to dig under the skin so deeply.

Standing there, my feet sinking a bit in the soft soil, I ached more than ever to return to my old life. And I told myself that what stopped me from acting was clear, and that all my attempts to make reality more complex paled before the obvious: my discovery of my mother's abandonment of me had to be what did me in. I shouldn't try to make the truth more mysterious than that. For a while my mother had been able to live without me. The important thing: my mother never changed her mind about me again after she came back for me. Her abandonment was temporary—that's what I must keep remembering. And that I had loved her beyond love. And that there was never anyone like her, and that she was wholly irreplaceable, as I was, finally, to her. What does it mean to give up what we love most? What does it mean to reclaim what we love most? Perhaps I have had to make myself know what such an experience is like? Or am I mystifying my life again? I suppose the obvious is mysterious enough.

The dark was settling. In fullest darkness the fireflies were meant to disappear. Until then, they sent across the air their flickering signals.

There was only one truly inexplicable mystery left, and I knew myself well enough to claim it: I would forgive Sofie.

❖

Acknowledgments

I'm grateful to the editors of the journals in which some of these stories have appeared previously, sometimes in different versions and under different titles: *Antioch Review, Ascent, Cezanne's Carrot, Confrontation, Freightstories, Gargoyle, Hotel Amerika, Idaho Review, Roanoke Review,* and *Short FICTION* (England).

"You Know You've Made It When They Hate You" first appeared in *Antioch Review* and was reprinted in *Peculiar Pilgrims: Stories from the Left Hand of God.*

I wish to thank Peter Conners for his insightful advice and his faith in this collection. I'm also grateful for the assistance of Jenna Fisher and the other dedicated people at BOA who have helped usher these stories into the wider world.

I thank my students and departmental colleagues at Lafayette College. My gratitude extends as well to Anthony Caleshu, Anna Duhl, Marilyn Kann, Neil McElroy, MaryAnn Miller, W. P. Osborn, Emily Schneider, Randy Schneider, Beth Seetch, Diane Shaw, Jim Toia, and Sylvia Watanabe.

I thank Yetta and Ted Ziolkowski, my inspiring and invigorating in-laws.

I write with the sustaining memory of the lives of my mother Rose, my father Charles, my brother Joe, my sister Lana, and my niece Carla.

This book is dedicated to my sister Alice Faye. No one could be more loyal or more thoughtful, more reliable, good-natured or, frankly, more organized. She should run continents. We would all be her delighted citizens.

My daughters Theodora and CeCe have given me the most gasping, head-on-the-knees laughter that a person could experience without losing consciousness. I cannot thank them enough for letting me listen to them and for being their uniquely and undeniably beautiful selves.

I thank my husband Eric—with love beyond words.

❖

About the Author

Lee Upton is the author of twelve previous books, including five books of poetry, four of literary criticism, a novella, and a recent collection of essays, *Swallowing the Sea: On Writing & Ambition, Boredom, Purity & Secrecy*. Among her awards and prizes are the Pushcart Prize, the National Poetry Series Award, and the Miami University Novella Award.

BOA Editions, Ltd. American Reader Series

Colophon

BOA Editions, Ltd., a not-for-profit publisher of poetry and other literary works, fosters readership and appreciation of contemporary literature. By identifying, cultivating, and publishing both new and established poets and selecting authors of unique literary talent, BOA brings high-quality literature to the public. Support for this effort comes from the sale of its publications, grant funding, and private donations.

The publication of this book is made possible, in part, by the special support of the following individuals:

Anonymous x 3
Jim Daniels
Anne Germanacos
Suzanne Gouvernet
Michael Hall
Sandi Henschel, *in honor of her daughter Sarah Piccione Sortino*
Jack & Gail Langerak
Barbara & John Lovenheim
Boo Poulin
Cindy Winetroub Rogers
Deborah Ronnen & Sherman Levey
Steven O. Russell & Phyllis Rifkin-Russell
David W. Ryon
Sue S. Stewart, *in memory of Stephen L. Raymond*
Kay Wallace & Peter Oddleifson

❖